Turkey John

Turkey John

by
Artie Whitworth

Illustrated by
Karen Watts

Ozark Publishing, Inc.
P. O. Box 228
Prairie Grove, AR 72753

iii

F
Whi   Whitworth, Artie
         Turkey John, by Artie Whitworth.
         Illus. by Karen Watts.
         Ozark Publishing, Inc., 1995.
         175P. illus.
         Summary: The setting for this story is a small rural town
         in southwestern Oklahoma during the Great Depression.
         Many struggled to survive, as did Turkey John, who lived
         in a dugout earthen house and fished and hunted for his
         livelihood.

ISBN Casebound 1-56763-190-8
ISBN Paperback   1-56763-191-6

Ozark Publishing, Inc.
P.O. Box 228
Prairie Grove, AR 72753
Ph: 1-800-321-5671

Printed in the United States of America

Dedicated to

the memory of J. L. Whitworth to whom I owe not only my existence, but most all of the moral standards by which I have lived throughout my lifetime.

Foreword

"Turkey John" was half-Cherokee Indian and half-Irish, but did not seem to fit either race. Hence, he chose a life alone. There on the river bank he seemed at peace. He wore a pair of cut-off pants and went barefooted, but was always in his wide-brim black hat. When he went into the nearest town for supplies, his hat would be decorated with a large turkey feather and a silver-studded band. He would also wear a hand-beaten silver bolo tie around his shirt collar and western-type boots. When he rode into town on his big black horse, he sat straight and tall in the saddle. Being the loner that he was, he took up fishing for his livelihood, living in a dugout earthen house and fishing from a homemade flat-bottom long boat. He took only the amount of fish from the river that he needed to sustain life. A pitcher pump with a rubber hose running down into the river supplied his water for cooking, drinking, bathing, etc. His trips to town were to replenish his supply of staple food, such as beans, flour, and sugar, but most of his food came from the wilderness, such as rabbit, squirrels, deer, and fish. The setting for the story is a small rural town in southern Oklahoma, but most of Turkey's customers came from miles around to buy his fish.

The events, places, and people in this book are all real. They have been fictionalized somewhat to make the story more readable and some of the names have been changed for their protection.

CONTENTS

Turkey John

Chapter I

SNOWBALL

I stood with my bare toes through the crack between the second and third rail of the board fence, looking over the top rail at the biggest hog I had ever seen in my life. Mr. Clark said it weighed over five hundred pounds. I don't know just how much five hundred pounds is, but I did know it was the biggest hog I ever saw. My little brother, Dick, who had climbed upon the fence beside me, just said, "Gosh!" I sure was glad Daddy wasn't there, for he sure didn't like that word. He always said it was just short for cussing. Our daddy was a big hand at Bible reading and stuff.

Dick and I stood there for the longest time looking at the big hog, when Leo climbed over and began to scratch the sow on her side. I couldn't believe what I saw. This giant hog just fell over like she had been shot with a rifle and lay still and quiet while Leo Clark scratched her side and belly. Leo was real proud of what he was showing us, and he kept cutting his eyes up at my big brother, Joe, to see if he was impressed. You see, Leo wasn't real good in very many things. He was the schoolmaster's son and had moved to our town when Mr. Clark took the job to be in charge of our school. When you are not one of the locals, it's hard to break right in and be one of the gang. But Joe, who was five years older than me, had taken a liking to Leo, and that's why we had asked to spend that Saturday at the Clarks' while Mother and Daddy went to the county seat to buy a month's supply of things. Leo saw that we were losing interest in the big hog, so he quickly said, "Let's go see the puppies," and over the hog-pen fence and into the barn he ran. Joe was right with him, and Dick and I were close behind.

Over in a pile of hay in the corner of a barn stall was Leo's dog. She had five puppies, three slick-haired dogs like herself and two balls of fur. One long-haired dog was a brown-black mixture, and one was snow white, except for a black spot around the left eye. Everyone picked up a puppy and began to play with them. I grabbed the snow-white one that had caught my eye right off. I had never seen a prettier pup. I rubbed his nose and wooled and shook him a bit, and he began to growl in make-believe combat, biting at my hand and catching my sleeve and hanging on. I had never had a dog before. Daddy didn't like "suck-egg dogs" because he was a chicken man. We always had lots of laying chickens and frying roosters and some big rooster to make chicken and dumplings out of. We also had one little tight-tit jersey cow and two goats. Daddy liked goat meat, so we always had one or two to clean up the weed patches and to butcher when they were ready. Right off, I knew this puppy should be called "Snowball," and I wished that Daddy didn't think every dog sucked eggs and that he would let me have one. Almost every boy in our little town had a dog. All the farm boys 'round about had a good squirrel and possum dog that would also go to the pasture and bring in the milk cows in the evening. Wendell, who lived across the road from us, even had a cow he could saddle and ride to help his dog bring up the milk cows.

All day Saturday we did things that four boys hard at play do. We even had a great corn-cob fight, and I got hit real hard just above the eye with a wet cob out of the hog pen. But all that day, my mind was on Snowball, and I wondered just how I would bring it up to Daddy and make him see how valuable a dog would be around our place.

With our bare feet making tracks in the dusty road home, I brought the subject up to Joe. He, being older, might just have some idea how we could pull it off.

He felt like our best bet would be the squirrel and rabbit route, for he knew how Daddy liked wild meat. He could always get Daddy's permission to go hunting with the sawed-off shotgun, even though he was the cause of the gun being sawed off to begin with. Joe had stuck the gun in a snowbank while crawling through a fence, then shot at a rabbit and blew the end of the barrel off. Daddy then cut it off with a hacksaw, making it a sawed-off gun. Now it was the best gun we had for rabbits because it shot such a wide pattern. You just couldn't miss a rabbit with it at close range.

That night just after family altar time when we knew Daddy would be in his most charitable frame of mind, we brought up the subject of a dog. Now family altar time at our house came after chores and supper were over. We also had some time to play checkers or some other game and perhaps pop some popcorn. Mother, in her little platform spindle rocker, would read the Bible by the light of a coal-oil lamp that set in the colonnade just beside her chair. Most of the time, little sister Emily was in Mama's lap. Then we three boys sat in cane- or goat-skin-bottom straight chairs, and Daddy sat in his big wide-arm wooden rocker. This completed the quarter circle around the living room. The room was large enough to have a bookcase, dresser, iron double bed, library table, fern stand, and another rocker beside the other colonnade where the table model Philco arch-shaped battery radio sat.

This particular evening I moved to the big rocker and sat on Daddy's leg while the Bible was being read. After prayer, with Mother leading first, then Daddy closing the prayer with a lot of thanksgivings, I quickly mentioned matter-of-factly that we sure needed a dog around the place. For you see, I knew that just as soon as Daddy quit praying, he would go to bed, and then there could be no noise or lights on in the house after that and certainly no family discussions. Joe quickly took up the talk about our need for a dog. A dog, he said, would sure help him bring home more rabbits and squirrels. He knew where there was some big swamp rabbits. If he only had a dog to help run them out of the brush piles, he could shoot them.

After we both had said all we could think of in favor of a dog, you could tell Daddy was deep in thought. We both waited without even breathing until Daddy decided to speak. "Well, boys, it sounds fine, but I don't know where we would get a good hunting dog. And I sure don't want an old egg-sucking hound bawling around the place."

Joe said, "Well, Mr. Clark has a fine cur dog that Leo said was a good squirrel and possum dog, and she has a litter of five. Mr. Clark said we could have the pick of the litter."

"Maybe Monday after school we could walk over there and look at them," Daddy said. (We don't make any business deals on Sunday, and that was understood by all without asking.)

That night three boys bounded up the stairs without any argument about going to bed so early and not getting to listen to the "Grand Ole Opry" on the radio. But sleep was hard to come by that night, for all three boys had their minds on a puppy dog.

After a time of whispering and one warning up the stairs, we got quiet.

As was my habit I took my two-cell flashlight from under my mattress and my book from under my pillow and began to read a chapter of *Call of the Wild*. That book had whetted my appetite for a dog in the first place. The flashlight routine was because Daddy didn't allow lights in the house after he went to bed. I had bought the light and batteries with my cotton-picking money, and Daddy didn't know I had it. The books I borrowed from the school library. This was a habit I developed after my second-grade teacher gave me the *Life of Teddy Roosevelt* as a reward for reading the most books in our class.

Sunday morning soon came, and everything on the place was fed and watered before Daddy and we three boys came in to a breakfast of hot biscuits, eggs, red-eye gravy, and homemade peach preserves. Then we all got ready for Sunday morning church at the Mission.

There were three churches in our town: the Baptist, the Methodist, and the non-denominational Community Mission. The Baptist didn't have a pastor and only met about once a month. The Methodist had been closed down for a long time and had made a dwelling house of their church building for a bedfast lady named Grannie Clifton. So the Mission was the only active church in town. That was mostly because my daddy served as janitor and pulpit committee and kept a preacher in the pulpit. There was really no regular pastor, just pulpit fills, traveling preachers, and revivalists. But we usually had a preacher. We all sang very loud from old paperback *Stamps Quartet* song books, when we were lucky enough to have one that didn't have that particular page torn out.

Actually the Mission was on a piece of our land. Daddy had built it and dedicated it to the Lord and the community.

This Sunday there was a goodly number of folks at the Mission. Several kids were there to share our good news that tomorrow we might get us a puppy. We were careful not to tell the possible source, for fear that someone might beat us to the pick of the litter. I had not given it a thought that Dick, or Joe, or even Daddy would select a puppy other than Snowball. He was for sure the pick of the litter.

After church Daddy invited the preacher home with us for dinner. We had beef roast, gravy, whipper-will peas, and mashed potatoes. We always had beef roast after my parents' monthly trip to the county seat. This great meal was topped off with Mama's peach cobbler with some of Tight-tit's, our old jersey cow's, cream over it. My, what a treat.

Even though the table talk was about church stuff and Sister So-and-So, who had gotten religion but hadn't quit her snuff and really needed all our prayers, I wasn't listening much. My mind was on

Snowball and how I could build him a bed on the back porch. I could use an old apple box that was in the barn and put some tow sacks and an old worn-out cotton sack in it. Perhaps Daddy would let me move it to the front porch, which faces south, and would keep the pup warm when it got real cold this winter.

Finally the table talk was finished. Everyone moved out to the front porch to enjoy the fall sun and fresh breeze from the southwest. All, that is, except Mama and me. It was my time to dry dishes. We boys took turns on this chore, and after several arguments, we finally put it down on the S&S Grocery Store calendar that hung on the kitchen wall. So there it was, a big H standing for my name, Hank, on Sunday, October 6. It wasn't until I looked at the calendar that I remembered that this coming Tuesday would be my birthday. Perhaps Daddy had that in mind when he so easily agreed to go look at Leo's puppies.

By the time I finished drying the dishes, a big game of kick-the-can was going on in our yard and barnyard area. There were about twelve kids in the game. Wendell from across the road was "It," and he had three boys in the pen (a circle drawn on the ground). Wendell was out looking for someone else to spot and yell his name and tell him to "shoot in my pen." I slipped out the front door and around to the east side, running through the pen and kicking the can as far as I could kick it. This released those in the pen. We ran around the front, to the west side, and hid in the blackberry patch. I could hear Daddy whipping his leg and laughing. One of his greatest delights was to watch kids at play.

Wendell, after he found the can and put it back in the circle, looked for us a while and then yelled something about the game being unfair and went home. This ended the kick-the-can game.

We all came in and decided we would dig holes and play roley-holey. Now roley-holey was a marble game whose rules are somewhere between the rules of croquet and golf. Four holes were dug with a spoon in a straight row, and a fifth hole was dug at a right angle from the fourth. Each boy, using his favorite shooting taw, would shoot to make the holes.

The game begins by "legging to a line" (that is, tossing your marble from the first hole back toward a beginning line some twenty feet away). The boy getting his marble closer to that line would be the first shooter; the second marble would be the second shooter, and so on. Then, beginning at the line, you shoot to make the first hole.

The best thing to dig the holes with was a certain table spoon that Mama had in the kitchen. I had to promise faithfully that I would bring it right back. If the dirt was dry and hard, we would have to use our barlow knife (which every boy owned and carried with him at all times) to pick up the dirt, and then the dirt was removed with the spoon. This was repeated until the required size of hole was made. The barlow knife was also handy for a quick game of knife plugging or mumbletypeg, which I won't explain at this time.

Soon the holes were dug, and the great game of roley-holey began. I was the third shooter. Every boy had his own unique shooting taw. Mine was a blue "cat's eye" agate. Most taws were glassies or crocks. To have a true agate was the envy of the whole town. I had plowed mine up in the garden. No one knew its history, but needless to say I was quite proud of it. With so many boys in the game, it was hard for anyone to win. Just about the time you would get within shooting distance of a hole, someone would hit your marble and knock it way out in the weeds. Or if you were behind a post or something and needed to move right or left a span, someone would see that and yell "venture anies." This meant you would have to shoot from where you were. So, after an hour or two, the game began to break up, and boys began to leave to go home and do chores before supper.

Everyone planned to go to the Mission that night for church. The older boys liked seeing the girls who would be there. We younger boys just liked getting together. Though during church, Dick and I never got to sit with the boys, because Daddy's rule was that we sit within the first three benches on one side of the center aisle or the other. It was very hard to get another boy to sit up that

10

close, because they couldn't talk up there.

When the other boys were all gone home, my brothers and I began our chores. The kitchen wood box had to be filled with cook wood which had been cut during the week (never on Sunday) from the ash and hackberry logs that had been hauled up from the ash flats down near the river bottom. The chickens had to be fed, and old Tight-tit had to be milked. Milking was Joe's job; feeding the chickens was mine; and Dick had to carry in wood. I would help him when the chickens were fed.

I stood in the corncrib door and yelled "hippo" as loudly as I could, and chickens came from all over the place. Six big ears of yellow-dent corn were shelled and thrown out among the chickens. I threw the cobs at the old red rooster who kept all the young roosters run back so they couldn't eat. He and I were always at war. He tried to spur me every time I was in the barnyard and he could catch me not looking. Our outhouse was down the other side of the barnyard, so one had to pass through there two or three times a day.

Soon the chickens were fed, and I had helped Dick load the wood box with wood and kindling for fire starting. Two buckets of water were drawn up from the well for the kitchen and back-porch wash stand. Joe had finished milking the jersey cow. The calf was turned in to finish the job and then kept in the stall for the night while Tight-tit was put back out in the lot. We all three washed our hands and faces on the back porch at the wash stand, with lye soap that Mama had made. We were ready for supper.

Supper was warmed-over roast and gravy with some fresh hot bread that Mama had baked. After Daddy prayed, we were very careful that the preacher was served first and that some food was left in case he wanted seconds. It wasn't until he had excused himself from the table that we could clean out the dishes, which we always did, especially when we had roast and gravy.

All of us then put on our "Sunday-go-to-meeting" clothes and went to the Mission. We always got there a little early to pick up trash, straighten the song books, and tidy up a bit. It was during that time that I thought of Snowball, and my heart nearly leaped into my mouth. I had clean forgot about him all afternoon. Tomorrow was the big day, and I hadn't even fixed him a bed yet.

I didn't hear much of Preacher Smith's sermon because I was thinking of Snowball. I wondered how old a dog had to be before you could teach him to tree a squirrel or possum? It was too close to winter now to count on him for possum hunting this year. I would have to rely on my steel traps for my winter spending money I got by selling furs. But surely, by spring, I could count on him for squirrel season. Then next year he and I would haul every possum out of those Teague woods.

Morning came, and school passed awfully

slow, but finally the school bell rang and I headed home, which was not very far to go as our back fence was the schoolyard fence. I took the back-porch steps with one bound, then went through the back door and stood in the middle of the kitchen floor asking Mama where everyone was. Dick, who was in the first grade, was soon standing beside me, and by Mama's instructions we both headed for the front porch. There we found Daddy and Joe in debate over perpetual motion. Joe, being in high-school science, liked talking about those big subjects, and Daddy delighted in seeing just how much Joe had learned and could reason on his own. I wasn't a bit interested in perpetual motion. There was only one subject that interested me, and that was a puppy dog named Snowball. So I quickly slipped my subject into the conversation.

Daddy said, "It will be a while before Mr. Clark will be home. He is the head of the school you know, and besides, those dogs aren't going anywhere. They will still be there when we get there, I am sure." And he laughed a big belly laugh. I am not sure whether he enjoyed my anxiety or his wisdom, but I sure wasn't going to ask. In a little while, Daddy, Joe, Dick, and I were on our way over to Mr. Clark's house.

There they were, five fine puppy dogs. I had already convinced Dick that Snowball was the pick of the litter. Joe knew my choice, though he had not come right out and said that he agreed with me. So we all three waited for Daddy to look them over one at a time. First, Daddy separated them into boys and girls, which none of us had even thought to do. There were two boys and three girls in the litter. That put Snowball and one motley-colored, slick-haired pup in the same group, for they were boy dogs. Daddy, without much delay, picked up the friskiest one, and that was Snowball. He handed him to me and said, "Happy Birthday," then gave one of his belly laughs, ending with a loud "whew." Mr. Clark, Leo, and everyone else laughed with Daddy. I found out some weeks later that Mama had already told Daddy which one was my choice. But nothing mattered then except Snowball and the fact that he was our dog.

Chapter II

HORSESHOE LAKE

Fall that year, in our little town, was about the same as other falls in the past, except these were troubled times. So many of our men were in the armed forces overseas fighting Germans and the Japs. We were in the midst of the awful World War II, which Daddy said made World War I look like a small battle. Each day in our town began with a gathering at Teague's store, where our post office was located.

The mail carrier made his daily route from the county seat. Then coming through each little town, he left a mail sack and picked up a sack which contained the community's carefully written letters on the thin onion-skin paper to loved ones in the war. The tension of the gathering would begin to rise as the sack was brought in and dumped on Mr. Bud's sorting table. His experience let him sort back certain letters to be given out at the very last.

First, he would pick out the onion-skin letters from the servicemen and put them in the locked mail boxes or call out the name of the addressee if it was a general-delivery letter. There would be squeals of delight, and after a silent once over, it was usually read aloud, so everyone at the gathering could enjoy the news. Many of the letters were cut up so badly by the American censors that there wasn't much left to read. The men were not allowed to mention anything about the war and where they were fighting. Several families had worked out a code system with their sons or husbands before they had left and could mark the giant map kept on their living room wall as to exactly where their men were fighting. Then they could listen each night to Mr. Gabriel Heatter or Walter Winchell on their battery radio and know what their men were going through.

After all the other mail had been given out, tension would again rise. For now came the two kinds of letters that the community dreaded. The first one was "Greetings from your Uncle Sam," telling the receiver they were to report for examination and induction into the service. The last mail were those letters that always began with "We regret to inform you . . . ," "missing in action," "taken prisoner," "wounded in action," etc. This was always bad news, and some mother or wife would break into sobs, and all of us would feel very sad because we were community. We had lots of windows in our town displaying gold stars, meaning someone of that household had given their life fighting for our freedom.

It had been a very dry fall, which was good

news for the peanut farmers. That allowed them to get their crops harvested without getting rained on. Rain was bad for peanuts after they were dug, and it also destroyed the peanut hay, which the farmers counted on to feed their cows during the winter. But dry weather also meant the ponds and water supplies for the cattle were drying up. We even heard that Horseshoe Lake, which was a lake filled by overflow water from Blue River in the spring, was drying up. Horseshoe Lake was one of our favorite fishing lakes.

Daddy said, "I will knit you boys a seine. You can take it to Horseshoe Lake and catch us a lot of fish." So he took cotton cord and his net knitting needle and began working. He was one of the few men in our country who could make nets and seines for catching fish.

By Saturday morning the seine was ready. It was one-inch mesh with lead sinkers on the bottom cord and wooden floats on the top cord, and it was about thirty feet long. We rolled it up and tied it on our bicycles, along with a couple of tow sacks to carry the fish home in, and headed for Horseshoe Lake about three miles away.

We arrived some thirty minutes later, and Joe and I set about cutting two good stiff poles for the seine with our barlow knives. Soon the seine was tied to the poles. We stretched it out and waded into the mud and water of the almost-dry lake. Dick was behind the net in the center to hold up the float line.

Joe and I were on each pole, making sure the poles touched the bottom so that the lead line would drag on the bottom. Excitement grew as we felt the fish bump into the seine.

On the first drag we had three large buffalo fish, some carp, several crappies, and a good-sized blue catfish, along with lots of small perch. We pulled out on the dry bank to take the fish out of the seine and put them in the tow sack. We tied the top of the sack with a large cord and put it back into the water to keep the fish alive. Then we began our second drag. We hadn't gone far when we found a large hole about sixteen feet across and deeper than we could walk.

Joe said, "Hank, that hole will be full of fish because they go to the deepest water, but our seine won't go down that deep."

So we dragged the seine out on the bank, and with Dick holding the sack, Joe and I began to dive down to where the fish were. By feeling along the bottom, as the water was too muddy to open our eyes, we would find a fish and stick his head into the mud until he settled down some. We would locate his gills and mouth, then with fingers firmly in the gills and mouth, we would bring him up and put him into the sack.

About my third trip down, I found a huge fish. I slipped my hands along his sides. He was about as long as I was tall, but I couldn't find his gills. He was a scaly fish, but not like any I had ever felt. His body was more round than a buffalo or carp, more like a catfish, but a catfish had smooth skin, not rough scales. Not having much air left to stay down long, I tried to force what I thought was his head into the mud. With great force from his tail, he drove himself forward through my grip, taking some of the hide off my hands on his way, and leaving a wake behind him when he left. He was the roughest fish I had ever felt. Joe said that he was, an alligator gar and could have bitten off my hand. This broke up the hand grappling right then and there, and we returned to our original plan of seining for fish. One time after that the gar got into our seine, so we slowed down a bit and let him turn and swim out. He swam down to the other end of the lake and left a large wake behind him as he went. After four or five more drags with the seine, we had all the fish in both sacks that we dared try to carry on our bikes. I had also gathered a large number of shiner minnows, crawfish, and small perch that I had a special purpose for when I got home.

Finally we got home with our heavy load of fish and wet seine. We were a long time cleaning fish. The fish with scales on them had to be scaled with a stiff butcher knife, while the catfish had to be skinned before they could be prepared for cooking. There were far more fish than we could eat before they spoiled, so we shared some with our neighbors. The remainder was cut up into small pieces and packed in pint jars. Mama put on a pressure canner full to cook and seal. These would be eaten this winter. They were used like canned salmon or mackerel, but tasted much better.

Packing the fish in a jar reminded me of what I was going to do with all the small fish I had brought home. I packed the small fish into a large gallon jar, covered them with water, and sealed the lid tightly. I then took the spade and dug a deep hole in the ground and buried the jar. After the weather turns cold and animal furs get heavy and prime, I planned to dig up the jar, and by tightly holding my nose, I would put a spoonful of the stink bait around every trap I set. An old possum just can't resist investigating the stinking fish smell, and then it would step into my trap. Each prime possum fur, if cared for rightly, would bring me two to three dollars. That's good winter spending money for a country boy. A coon hide is worth about twice that much, and a mink hide will bring as much as twenty-five dollars. Skunk hides are also worth quite a bit, but I can't hold my nose long enough to skin one, so I just pass on old striped back. The only time I will even kill one is when he gets into the chicken house and begins to kill our chickens. Once one starts that, he will get a chicken every night until they are all gone.

My, how Daddy and all of us enjoyed that cat-fish and buffalo fish for supper. Daddy, who had raised another family and then his first wife died, had married my mother. We were his second family. He was now too old to go out and kill game and catch fish; so he had taught us boys how to bring home table meat. He dearly loved wild meat. He had enjoyed the fish supper so much that he let us stay up far past his bedtime and listen to almost all of the "Grand Ole Opry" on the radio. Finally we boys turned it off and went upstairs to bed. I was even too tired to read a chapter in my book, so the flashlight and book were not gotten from their hiding place that night.

October was rapidly coming to an end. I had been making some extra money on Saturday scrapping cotton (that is picking cotton in fields that had already been picked but new cotton had opened up since it was picked). The end of October was highlighted by Halloween celebration. This was a little different in our town. In the cities, the kids celebrated by what they called "trick or treating" but we wouldn't do that; we just tricked.

We boys had decided that we would "ticktack" Mr. Payne's house. Now ticktacking was done by tying a pin onto a long string and hooking the pin into a window screen. We would put rosin on the string, then rub the string with a damp handkerchief that would vibrate the string and make a great roaring noise inside of the house. If one didn't have the rosin, a damp string would work pretty well.

Mr. Payne went to bed early, so there was no problem pinning the string into the window screen.

Our string was long enough that we could get out in the pasture away from the house and hide in the weeds. We rubbed it a couple of times, then waited. Soon a light came on in a back bedroom. Mr. Payne walked through the house, but finding nothing he soon went back to bed. We waited until he was back in bed with the light out, and we rubbed the string again—this time extra hard. Mr. Payne lit the lamp again, and this time he came out the back door. We lowered the string so that he would not walk into it when he came around the house, but he found it anyway. We all ran across the pasture as hard as we could go, laughing all the way. We gathered at Wendell Teague's house, where his mother had made popcorn balls and candied apples. So we did the trick and got the treat, after all.

Chapter III

THE MISSION FIRE

October was gone, and Thanksgiving was soon upon us. All the ducks and Canadian geese had made their journey south. Jack Frost had been showing himself almost every morning. It had even snowed lightly once. In southern Oklahoma, snow sure makes kids excited. This snow wasn't even enough to put milk, sugar, and vanilla in for some snow ice cream. Snowball was growing fast, and he and I were becoming real pals. He was making a fine dog, but was losing his snow-white coat, and I could see little black spots appearing near his skin, especially on his back. But no way would I change his name.

I had already taught Snowball to catch a chicken and hold it until I told him to turn it loose. This is a great help in rounding up chickens that fly over the chicken-yard fence. After Snowball and I caught the chickens, Daddy would clip about two inches of feathers off one wing and put the chicken back in the chicken-yard. They are unable to fly out again for a year, until they grow new wing feathers.

Chickens are like some people; only a few of them are adventurous enough to try to fly over the fence to explore new worlds. Most are content scratching the same old dirt, eating and drinking whatever someone hands out to them. I kinda felt sorry for the adventurous chickens, but if I left them out, a skunk or civic cat (miniature skunk) would get them for sure.

Speaking of skunks, I set my traps in Teague's woods after school, and I needed to go run them. Teague's woods are the closest woods to my house and have plenty of possums in them. I am the only trapper who bothers with the woods so close to town. I was anxious to see how well my Horseshoe Lake bait works on possums. So I got up real early to run my traps. I only set four traps, but that would be all the time I would have to set and run traps before and after school.

The trip to the woods wasn't long at all. I guess it's because I trotted all the way. The first trap was in the persimmon thicket just before you get to the woods. Some persimmons were still on the trees, and I knew how possums like persimmons. Sure enough, there he sat in my trap, grinning at me.

Possums, unlike other wild animals, won't fight a trap. They just sit there and wait on you. A mink will even chew off his own foot to escape a trap. That's why you trap them in or near water; they will fall into the water and drown themselves. They can't swim with a trap on their foot.

I put the possum in my tow sack, pulled up the stake that held the trap chain, and threw the trap and chain over my shoulder to head across the creek to set number two. The trap was thrown, but there was no possum. When I checked the tracks, it was a bobcat or a very large house cat. I had heard of a big old wild tow cat in these woods, but I had never seen him. I pulled the stake and threw the trap over my shoulder and headed for the third set. There another possum sat, grinning like the first one. I dropped him in the sack after I released him from the trap. The fourth trap had a half-grown possum in it, no good for fur, but it would make Daddy awfully happy. He likes nothing better than rubbing a dressed young possum with black pepper and salt and baking him to a golden brown in the oven. I have to confess, I kinda like them myself, even though most folks would say, "You mean you eat possum?" When I got home it was almost school time, and Daddy offered to skin and stretch my two possum hides for me. I was glad for the offer because I hated to leave them in a sack all day while I was at school.

When I came home from school, I checked my hides. Daddy had done a good job stretching them and had hung them in the well house. After a couple of days, I'll scrape all the oil out of them and let them finish curing before I ship them to Sears and Roebuck. Daddy had used a couple of last year's stretching boards. If I continue to do good and my Horseshoe Lake bait continues to work, I will have to make some new boards. I also want to trap Halls Creek, which is north of town. I know there will be possums there. The very best possum woods are east of town and south of the cemetery, but Harry Jones and his dad trap those woods. They ship lots of hides every year. Of course, the most hides are shipped by Mr. Fox Burns. He is a professional trapper and traps the sloughs and flats in Red River bottom. He rides horseback to run his traps and majors on coons and mink. He also catches red and gray fox. That's how he got his nickname of Fox.

I had hid my bait in the woods the day before in a hollow stump so I wouldn't have to carry it back and forth. I had brought my traps home to wash and oil them. I didn't want possum scent on my traps when I reset them. After I cleaned and oiled my traps, then off to the woods I'd go. It isn't good to reset in the same place where you made a catch the day before, but I did reset in the persimmon thicket. I covered the trap with loose dry leaves and then sprinkled it good with stink bait. After I finished the set, I headed for the creek to set number two.

I heard something in the leaves ahead of me, but it was moving so fast I didn't get a look at it. Perhaps it was the big wild house cat. Snowball would have given him a run for his money, but I didn't bring my dog to trap set for fear he will get his foot in a trap. My traps aren't strong enough to break a bone or anything like that, but it wouldn't feel very good on his foot, I'm sure.

As I came to the creek, I caught a glimpse of movement on a log that had fallen into the creek, part in the creek and part out of the creek. I stopped dead still and watched. Sure as I am alive, there was a mink. One mink usually means two, but I never saw the other one. Boy, what I could do with a couple of twenty-five-dollar checks from Sears for mink hides. I needed a new winter Mackinaw coat for school, and extra money would be good about Christmas time. For the time being though, I would just have to settle for possum hides, as I don't know very much about trapping mink.

Perhaps when Uncle John comes to see us, he will teach me about trapping mink. There isn't much that Uncle John doesn't know. He is not really my uncle but my step-grandfather, but I was not taught to call him grandfather, just Uncle John. The people for miles around knew him as "Turkey John." He was a half-Indian who had become a commercial fisherman on Red River. He lived in dugouts and tents. My grandmother had left him because she didn't like his way of life. Also, Uncle John was a heavy drinker. There wasn't anything he didn't know about animals and fish. I have seen him talk wild squirrels down a limb almost to him. Birds didn't seem to be afraid of him, either. He always had his live boxes full of fish of every kind to sell.

The mink ran into a hole on a limb about three feet up from the trunk of the log. I was sure that's where his den was. The hole in the limb would put him above the watermark when the creek was up, and I was sure there would be another opening somewhere up the bank for a quick escape if he needed it. I didn't disturb him, for fear that human scent would cause him to move his den. Instead I crossed the creek about thirty yards down. I set my second trap on the bank under a large oak that had a big hollow opening about ten feet above the ground, a likely possum den if I ever saw one.

Soon I had all four sets made. I put my Horseshoe Lake bait back in the hollow stump and headed for home. The chickens had to be fed. And both cook- and heating-stove wood had to be carried in, along with the cobs and chips for fire starting. Coal oil cost a dime a gallon at Land's store. So Daddy was very careful not to use very much, just enough to get the dry corncobs to burning. Then the burning cobs in turn would light the wood. Dry ash wood was the easiest to catch fire and burned very hot, but it doesn't last long. Oak wood is usually added for lasting fire.

After supper we played some games of checkers and dominoes, with Joe winning most of the games. Then it was time for family devotions and bed.

It seemed like I had hardly gone to sleep, after reading a chapter in my book, when there was a strong knock at the front door and someone excitedly yelling J. L., J. L., which was what everyone called my dad. His name was really Joseph Lewis, but he just went by his initials. I could tell by the voice that it was Bo Duncan's dad. They lived on the Hall place just across the field, north of the schoolhouse.

When Daddy reached the front door, Mr. Duncan said, "J. L., the Mission is on fire." Hearing that, we boys leaped out of bed and had our overalls on and were down the stairs as quickly as possible. Daddy instructed us to get the two-wheeled cart that we used to haul wood from the wood lot and to take a washtub and bucket and fill up the tub from the rain barrel.

We were out the gate and headed for the Mission in hardly no time at all. Daddy and Mr. Duncan were pulling burning boards from the outside wall near the center of the blaze and kicking away the wood that someone had piled up against the Mission wall. We boys began to throw water on the flame, and we just about had it under control when we ran out of water.

I remembered that the road ditch at the end of the field west of the Mission usually had water in it, as I had caught lots of crawfish out of that ditch. So I headed that way with the cart. Sure enough, there was water in the ditch. Dick and I soon had the tub filled and were headed back. We dashed the water on the fire and burning coals until it was all out. Dad was very broken, because it was apparent that someone had piled dry wood against the Mission and set it on fire. We had no idea why someone would do that.

The next afternoon we hauled lumber from the house on the same wood cart, and Daddy repaired the big hole in the Mission wall. I still couldn't understand why someone would do such a thing. Daddy had instructed us to be careful and not tell anyone it was deliberately set on fire. The hole caused by the fire could be seen from the school grounds, and they all had decided that Daddy had left a lantern burning Sunday night and that's what had set the Mission on fire.

Two nights later, Daddy was awakened by a red glow in the western window. The Mission was on fire on all four sides. By the time we got there, the roof was caving in. We were not even able to salvage the song books. Daddy said they had used gasoline this time. We were all saddened, and Daddy had us all go home. He stayed to do some tracking. He returned home about an hour later. I heard him tell Mama he had tracked the man right to his front door. But Daddy was a great believer in justice in the world to come and everything doesn't have to be made right down here, so he didn't even report it to the sheriff's office.

It was this same way of thinking that had caused Daddy to close his grocery store during the depression and come home bankrupt. He had let the people buy food on credit until the shelves were empty because he knew their families were hungry. But knowing their situation, he had not required any of them to pay what they had owed. Daddy never asked one of them for payment even after the depression was over. Most all of them forgot they owed Daddy any money. If Daddy ever held a grudge or had hard feelings toward others, he never let it show. I only hope that when I grow up, I can learn how to forgive people as well.

Chapter IV

THE BLACK POSSUM

The garden was all in now, and what we didn't eat fresh was canned in jars for the winter. The last scrappings of the garden were made into large pots of garden soup and also canned. The popcorn and jumbo peanuts were harvested and put into the metal-lined wooden box in the barn, free from the mice. The field corn lay piled in the corncrib to feed the chickens and cow through the winter months. Even the garden had been raked and burned to kill all possible weeds and grass seeds that might come up and hinder our garden next spring.

The orchard fruit was all gone now, and the orchard had been raked and plowed. Daddy didn't like volunteer fruit trees coming up in his orchard, even though one of our best peach trees came up volunteer. It was a cross between an Alberta and an Indian peach and was the biggest and sweetest peach in our orchard.

Saturday came and the only major chore was to cut and split enough wood for the week. That would take an hour or so. Daddy kept our crosscut saw real sharp, along with the double-bit ax. Joe, Dick, and I lifted a log into the saw rack, made of four poles in the ground crossing in two X's about five feet apart. With the log in the rack, two of us would saw while the other would split the blocks with the ax. Cook wood was cut sixteen inches long and split into very fine sticks. Heating wood was cut twenty-four inches long, and a block only made about four sticks.

After the wood was cut and stacked, we were free for the day. Joe was going to Billy Wayne Smith's house for the day, but Dick and I were going to the cemetery woods. We were to meet several other boys there to build a log cabin for a clubhouse. I took the ax, with a warning from Daddy to be careful with it and be sure not to cut into a nail or wire. We tied the ax on our bike, and off we went riding double. We only had one bike to share. It was a Hawthorne we had gotten for Christmas last year. It was one of the finest bikes in town. We even had a speedometer on it to tell us how far and how fast we were going. I did the pumping, and Dick rode sidesaddle on the bar in front of me. Snowball was close behind, as he loved to go with us on our adventures.

After a ride through town and one stop at Jerry's house to find out that he had already gone on, we arrived at the gate, just south of the cemetery, that led into the woods. After we had passed through the gate, there was a well-defined path through the woods. Miss Rudolf, our first- and second-grade schoolteacher, lived just the other side of the woods and walked to and from school every day down that path. Also, the Shast and Rollins boys used that path to school and to town.

· When we arrived at the site where the cabin was to be built, Jerry, Ed, Harry, and Fonze were already there and busy at work clearing the land for the cabin. We were locating the cabin across the creek and in the thickest part of the woods where it could not be seen from the path through the woods or from the road that went south of the cemetery into Red River bottom. Axes were in motion and chips were flying. Dick and I untied our ax from the bicycle and joined the work crew.

Most of the timber was oak or elm and a little hard to cut. But it wasn't long until the land was cleared and the first logs were in place to form the outline of the cabin. We notched them just right for the second layer of logs and set about cutting them to length and notching them to fit. It would take all hands to lift each log into place. One log after another, the walls went up, leaving only one opening for a door. We weren't sure just how one would go about making a window. Besides, we agreed that we didn't want people looking in on our secret meetings.

After the walls were as high as we could reach, we cut smaller poles to form our roof. We knew where there was an old house falling down on the Williams' place. There we could borrow a few 2x4's to nail across to hold the roof poles in place and to nail the roof to. This old house was called the Clyde Barrow house because Bonnie and Clyde, the notorious bank robbers, used it as a hideout once. We not only got 2x4's but also got enough wide boards for the ends of our cabin under the roof. Ed's grandmother gave us a stack of rusty tin for our roof. Using Jerry's grandfather's wagon and team of mules (their names were Huldy and Jude), we loaded the tin and returned to the cabin site.

We used clay from the creek bank and filled all the cracks between the logs, except for one short place on the north, east, and west sides for lookouts. We had the door on the south side to peek through. We then put up a sheet-iron heater and stovepipe that we had found in the town dump. We were in business.

While we were in the creek getting clay, Snowball amused himself digging in the creek bank under some tree roots. I had forgotten about him, as I was so completely involved in the cabin building, until I heard him bark like he was serious about something. I ran to the creek and found him still at the same place, only now he had dug himself completely back into the bank, almost out of sight. I could hear the growl of some kind of animal in there with him.

I pulled Snowball out by the leg so I could

get a look at the animal. It was coal black, and I thought it must be a skunk, yet there was no odor. I looked again and he had turned around where I could see his face. The grin was unmistakably a possum. I had never seen a black possum before! I know that now and then there is a white one with pink eyes, but never had I heard of a black one. Over close to Blue River there is a den of black and white squirrels, so I guess anything is possible. This was a huge possum, much bigger than I had been catching in my traps.

I cut a green willow stick with a Y-fork close to one end. While I was cutting the pulling stick, Snowball went right back into the hole with the possum, and all the growling and scrapping began again. I had me a possum dog, for sure. Though he was just a pup, I knew he was enjoying the fight. I had to pull him out again, and one of the other boys held him while I slipped my stick with the Y-fork in past the possum and turned it. This slipped the Y-fork over his head and around his neck. Slowly I pulled him out until I could get him by the foot. Usually, I would use a barbed-wire twist for this, but I didn't want to damage the fur. When I got hold of his tail, I bumped him pretty hard against a tree, and he went into his sulling act. This is the possum's main defense. He wants you to think he is dead so that you will leave him alone.

Not having a tow sack, I took the cord from my bike that I had used to tie the ax on with. I tied the possum's feet together, then slipped his legs over the handlebar. With Dick holding the ax and watching the possum to make sure he didn't wake up and take a bite out of his leg, we peddled home as fast as we could go. I forgot about the cabin and everything else.

This black possum would surely bring us a premium, but Daddy didn't know what he would be worth. He encouraged me to do a good job pelting and stretching the fur. He was sure I would get an extra premium check for this possum.

We had to cut a new board because none of my boards was big enough for this black possum. Each day I worked with the hide to remove every bit of flesh and fat. Finally he was ready to ship. Even though I had other hides to ship, I wrapped and mailed the black by himself. I put a tag inside the package stating it was a black possum in case they didn't notice, as you stretch and ship possum hides inside out.

Several days passed, and Christmas would soon be upon us. I had not forgotten the black possum hide, but other things were now very important. One was that Land's store was selling fireworks. Other areas of the country celebrate the Fourth of July with fireworks, but in southern Oklahoma it is an important part of our Christmas celebration. We boys were shooting cans with Blackcat firecrackers. We would punch a hole in the bottom of a can, then bury the can (open end down), with about half of the can in the dirt. We would then slip the firecracker into the hole and light the fuse, dropping the firecracker through the hole into the can. When the firecracker went off, it would shoot the can into the air. The height of the shot depended on the tightness of the dirt packed around the can. If you packed it too tight, it wouldn't go very high, but if it was too loose, it would just kinda fall over. Each boy wanted his can to go the highest. A lot of arguments came out of this game, because there is no true way to measure the height the can travels.

We were busy shooting cans when I heard my brother Joe yell my name from Teague's store. Knowing that Teague's store was where our post office was located, my heart leaped into my mouth and I was thinking Sears Roebuck and my black possum. I ran to meet Joe, and he held out an envelope. I took it and looked at it. Sure enough, it was from Sears and was one of those envelopes with the window in it. I had gotten them before for furs I had shipped. Quickly I opened it with my barlow knife and found two checks made out to me. One was for three dollars for the large hide, and the other was a check for five dollars premium for "color and care." I was very happy. I ran back to get my bike and share the good news with my friends, then I headed home to tell Daddy. My Christmas was made now. I could buy the presents I wanted for my family and for the girl whose name I had drawn in our gift exchange in the fourth grade. I would even have some money left over. Surely, this was going to be a great Christmas.

Chapter V

THE COMMUNITY TREE

One of the big events in our town was the annual cake walk and pie supper. This raised money for the community Christmas tree. All the ladies of the community baked cakes and made a special pie. Everyone for miles around came to enjoy the evening and the special baking of the ladies of the community. Woe be to the husband or boyfriend who did not bid the highest and buy that special pie to eat with that favored lady. There were always those who would bid the price of the pie up just for the fun of it, even pooling their money together to do it.

First, a large double circle was drawn on the school gym floor with chalk. This double circle was then divided into sections large enough for two people to stand in. Each section was then numbered. Each section was filled by a couple who paid a dime to be there. Music was played by a local country music group while the couples walked around the circle. When the music stopped, each couple would be standing on a numbered section.

Then a number was drawn from a hat, and the couple standing on the winning number would receive a large portion of a fresh-baked cake to enjoy together.

We boys were allowed to also stand on a number if we could find a friend who had a nickel. I had been a winner twice already this time and was full of cake. I won once with my brother Dick and once with one of the Carter girls who lived about two miles southwest of town. Now, full of cake, my interest searched for something else to do. I went over to watch the Songman family make music. Mr. Songman asked me to fill in on the second guitar, as his girl needed a break. He knew I played rhythm guitar some, if they played in G, C, or D. My older brother, Joe, owned a Kay guitar, and I had used a "Learn to Play" book from XERF radio station in Del Rio, Texas, to learn how to chord. I got to practice some with Mr. Jeff Daniels, who lived next door just west of us. He played a fiddle and taught me how to hear chord changes and timing.

While I was playing, one of my friends came into the gym and told me that the new boy from California was outside bragging that he was going to whip me. He was trying to establish himself as the tough guy in town, I guess. Why he decided that I would be the one who could make his name as a tough guy, I don't know. He was taller and larger than I, but I was a year older than he. His name was Larry, and his grandfather owned the only honkey tonk in our area.

42

After I played for a while, the guitar player returned and took my place. I decided I had better go outside and meet this challenge. When it came down to it, I thought he would back down. Seven boys who had been watching to see what I was going to do fell in behind me with words of encouragement. Outside, Larry and two or three of his friends he had with him to watch him back me down walked to meet me. Even though it was a might cold, Larry had his jacket off and his sleeves rolled up so we could see his muscled arms. He did have about four inches reach on me, for I am short and stocky built. He doubled his fist and did a little dance like a bantam rooster, then snorted and thumbed his nose like he was the prize fighter Joe Louis or Billy Conn or Tommie Farr.

Now, my daddy had taught me not to fight unless it is forced upon me but to always defend myself. Just in case I had figured Larry wrong, I decided my best defense was a quick offense. So before he had time to think, I plowed into him. I hit him twice, locked him into a clinch, and threw him to the ground. When he was on his back, I put both knees into his arm muscles, which made his arms useless. He bucked and pitched a couple of times, but decided I had him pinned and settled down. Tears formed in his eyes, which let me know he had had enough. Everyone was yelling, "Hit him again while you have him down," but I decided perhaps that would not be fair fighting, and I always want to be known as someone fair. I just held him there. Finally I asked him if he had had enough, and he said very softly, "Yes."

I said, "I don't believe I heard you clearly, Larry." Then he came back with a loud, "YES," that everyone could hear. When I let him up, he went home bawling like a baby. I didn't know at the time, but he told his granddad I had jumped him in the dark and had given him a whipping. He did have a little mouse under one eye where I hit him. I had to deal with his grandfather later, but that is another story.

I straightened my clothes as best I could and returned to the gym as if nothing had happened. But my friends couldn't keep it quiet and told everyone that I had whipped Larry Hunt and that he had started the fight. The cake walk was still going on, except now they were giving away whole cakes to each winner. The ladies of the community had brought many cakes, and it was now time for the pie supper. Soon all the cakes were gone, and the people were called to the front for the auction of the pies.

The first pie was Opal's, the grass widow (what the locals call a divorced lady). Opal had several men friends, so the bidding went up fast. Her pie was sold off for seven dollars. Then one pie after another was auctioned off by Mr. Songman. Billy Joe James was home from the service because of a Purple Heart (wounded in action). With his

44

mustering-out pay, he was having a lot of fun running up the bidding on all the pies. One pie even sold for eighteen dollars to a young farm boy who was sweet on one of the town girls. That would have been several days cotton-picking or peanut-threshing money, which was very hard money to make.

All the pies were sold in a little while. A total for the cake walk and pie supper income was counted and given to be almost four hundred dollars. This was the biggest it had ever been, even with all the missing men who were off fighting in the war. There was a deep sense of caring for those families whose men were away or who had lost men in the war. I guess that is one of the good things about living in the country. It seems the people there go out of their way to help each other.

Before everyone went home, a date was set for the community Christmas tree. Some men were to meet and cut the tree and set it up on the Saturday before Christmas. The school board was given the job of buying the treats for the sacks. The schoolteachers were to make a list of each family and of the number in the family. A date was set to sack the treats, and several promised to help do that. They were to be sacked the day before that night so the candy wouldn't all stick together. This was the date I was interested in. Living next to the schoolyard had some real advantages. I could always be there when important things happened–like sacking candy. When the sacks are all full, there are always some odd pieces of candy left or an odd apple or orange or some nuts, and these are shared by the workers.

Saturday, December 16, soon came. I watched all morning for the arrival of the Christmas tree. Mr. Dunegan and his boys were to cut it down on Cedar Ridge, near the bluff of Red River, and bring it in a wagon. Just after dinner (the noon meal), they came through the west gate of the schoolyard. I believe it was the biggest tree we had ever had. It hung out of the back of the wagon farther than the length that was in the wagon. To keep it in the wagon they had tied it down with a lariat rope. I ran across the schoolyard and was there to help unload the tree. Our trouble, though, was getting the tree through the double door in the front of the gym. We had to trim some of the lower limbs off, and then we pulled with all our might to get it through.

By that time several other men had showed up and helped us put the base on the tree and stand it up in the gym. To make sure it remained standing, we tied the top of it to the cross beams that held up the gym roof. Our gym was a WPA-built gym and was made very strong. The WPA was President Roosevelt's work program to help relieve the nation's depression. Many of the men of the community had worked on the gym during the depression to earn a living for their families.

When the tree was up, several ladies came in

to do the decorating. I stayed on to help, for some-one had to climb the tall ladder to decorate the top branches, and the angel would have to be put on from the roof beams.

Before I knew it, the sun was getting low and my chores had to be done. The sun goes down quickly in December, and now it is already the six-teenth. Christmas would come before you know it. My only worry was my part in Monday night's Christmas program. My teacher decided we need-ed something patriotic in the program because the war was still going on. Being good at memorizing, I was to give Lincoln's Gettysburg Address. I had to wear a stovepipe hat and a black coat and stand on a stump that she had made from a piano stool wrapped in some brown paper. It wasn't the mem-orizing that worried me, I had all that OK. Standing on that stool and trying to look like Lincoln while I said all that "Three score and ten years ago" stuff in front of all the people was what had worried me. If you think there was a crowd at the cake walk, well, no one would miss the Christmas tree if they could help it at all.

I quickly ran home and fed the chickens and filled the wood boxes. Joe and Dick came in about that time, and Dick helped me get the cobs and chips for kindling while Joe milked the cow. Our supper was red beans, fried potatoes, and hot corn bread. It was the meal that we repeated more than any other. But we boys really didn't mind it at all.

The table talk was about Christmas. Emily wanted a doll. Dick and I had asked for a caterpillar tractor we had found in the Sears Christmas catalog. Joe wanted a motor for a model plane that he was building–one that would really make it fly.

I had brought home a handful of shiny lead foil icicles left over from last year's community tree. They had bought new ones for this year's tree. We decided to put up our own tree that night. Joe and Dick had cut one today and brought it home from Williams' pasture. They had also cut a large limb of red berries for stringing. I would pop some corn for stringing, too. Mama would get the box of decorations from the attic, the box that we had carefully stored last year. Emily helped me string berries and corn, and Joe and Dick put a base on the tree so it would stand up. Daddy just watched and gave advice as usual.

By family devotions time we were all finished. The tree looked great. It stood right in front of the big window in the living room.

Everyone then went to special hiding places and brought the packages that had already been wrapped. Mama pinned the Christmas cards our family had received around the colonnade, and we hung the crepe-paper bells on the ceiling in the center of the room. Those small bells had been in our family as long as I could remember. We would make some paper ropes to hang from each corner of the room to the other bells at a later time.

We all admired our work, and Mama took the Bible and read about how excited Mary was that Christmas was coming and that she was going to be the Mother of the Christ. After prayer, we all went off to bed.

Monday night, December 18, finally arrived. The people had already begun to gather by the time I got my chores done. I hurriedly got ready for the big night of the community Christmas tree, then dashed out the back gate and across the schoolyard to the gym. Instead of a big area for a cake walk, the gym was set up with folding chairs in front of the stage. The tree was in the corner of the gym, all decked out in Christmas decorations and laden with presents and brown paper bags filled with treats. The sacks, which I had helped sack, were filled with two red apples, two oranges, Brazil nuts, English walnuts, hazel nuts, orange slices, chocolate drops, and Christmas ribbon candy. The only time we saw most of these treats was at Christmas.

The program was presented one grade at a time. By the time the third grade was finished, I had my stovepipe hat and split-tailed coat on. When it came my time, the stump was moved out in the center of the stage. I was very careful to mount the stool, because it was one of those stools that screw in and out to raise and lower the seat. I did not want to fall off that thing in front of all those people. When I was firmly planted on top of the stump, I drew myself to full height and tried to look like Lincoln. This was hard, as I am not very tall. I was about to the middle of the Gettysburg Address when someone outside set off a red-devil screamer and a whole package of Blackcat firecrackers. I almost swallowed my tongue, and, of course, everyone laughed. When I finally got my senses back, I continued my speech.

Finally, when all the classes had finished and the high school had presented a one-act Christmas play, we all crowded onto the stage and led the crowd in some Christmas carols. Our final song was "Here Comes Santa Claus" and while we were singing, the gym door burst open and in walked a motley looking Santa, yelling, "Ho, ho, ho!" Everyone knew it was Botley Whitmore, but no one seemed to care. Nor did they care that his red suit was the same one he had used since before the war began. The excitement was very high, especially among the children who had left their seats and crowded around Santa. They knew that the black bag he had around his waist was filled with candy. He first began to hand each child a handful of candy, but decided that would take too long, so he began to throw handfuls of it among the kids.

The jolly old elf then moved to the big Christmas tree and with the help of the school-teachers and superintendent, he began to hand out individual gifts from those piled under the tree. Almost every child got at least one gift, and if a child didn't get a gift, somehow the news was whispered back to Santa and he just happened to have one for them over behind the tree. He was in such a hurry trying to work in all the before-Christmas trips, he just didn't have time to write names on every kid's gift. Christmas is one time that even the most devout will allow a little fibbing, especially by Santa Claus.

Soon all the gifts were given out. Then each family's name was read from a list, along with the number in the household. Brown paper bags of treats were delivered to the head of the family for each member. Daddy didn't come, so Joe received the six sacks for our family and one for Turkey John.

When Santa was all finished and had slipped out and on his way, we all sang "Silent Night." This seemed to bring meaning to the whole evening. Even Hoss Amborne, the town clown, was serious for those few minutes. Mr. Clark took charge and thanked everyone for coming and announced that school would be out until January 2. All the kids whistled and applauded, and Mr. Clark wished everyone "a very merry Christmas" and dismissed us to go home.

The schoolyard was turned into a fifteen-minute fireworks display, with lots of Blackcats, red-devil screamers, roman candles, bottle rockets, and an occasional cherry bomb. Even the men of the community got in on this celebration. The horses and teams of mules tied to the schoolyard fence got real disturbed during this part of the celebration. We didn't have very many cars in our town then, and most all the farm folks traveled by horseback or wagon.

When the fireworks were over, everyone went home. Joe, Dick, and I crossed the schoolyard and went through the back gate to our house. Emily had gone home earlier and had watched the fireworks from our back porch with Daddy and Mama. When we got there, Daddy opened his sack and took out an orange slice and a chocolate drop. He had no teeth, except those in the dining-room safe, which he could never wear, so he could only eat the soft candy.

A few days after the Christmas program, Uncle John (Turkey) came by our house, and we gave him his sack. He brought gifts for all of us. We three boys got a handmade bow and arrow. They were made from bow-darc (bois d'arc). This was the toughest wood grown in North America and was known by the Indians for its value in making bows. The older the wood gets, the tougher it gets. The fence post in the corner of our yard was bow-darc and had been there over forty years. Other than the hole where bluebirds nested each year, it was as sound as a dollar. Uncle John brought Emily a doll made of cloth and stuffed with cotton, and he brought Mama three yards of material for a new dress. He wanted Mama to also make a little dress for Emily's doll out of the scraps of the material. Daddy got a new netting needle made of bow-darc that held lots of twine on the spool. He also got a request from Turkey John to make him three double-throated fish nets. Uncle John would cut the dogwood and make the hoops for the nets.

Uncle John stayed two days with us, but knowing my daddy wouldn't let him stay if he was drinking, two days was all he could last without whiskey. During those two days he and my dog, Snowball, became real good friends. I never knew of an animal that didn't like that half-Indian man. He just had a way with animals. He stayed all the next day in town in Hunt's honkey tonk drinking. When he left town late that evening, he was riding his big black horse. You could hear him calling turkeys almost a mile away, as he rode down into Red River bottom. That is where he got his name Turkey John.

Folks always wondered how Turkey John kept such a noble horse to ride. It wasn't always the same horse, either. He would sell his horse to pay his commercial fishing-license fee or to buy his winter's supply of food and clothing. A few months later you would see him riding another beautiful animal. He told me once that there was still a small herd of mustangs that ran the river bottom. This was possible because there was still some free range left along the river. Some years before I was born, we had a great flood. It was in 1927, I believe. It rained for days, and the river came so far out of bank, it was from bluff to bluff, more than two miles wide. After the river went back, it had moved its channel south almost a mile. This gave Oklahoma a strip of land a mile wide and about fifteen miles long that was not on the Oklahoma survey records, so no one really owned it.

In this strip of land a herd of mustangs ran. They were mavericks lead by one noble stallion and some mares he had stolen at night from the farms and ranches along the river bottom. This no-man's-land was where Turkey John lived and roamed. It was just the place for a half-breed Indian who couldn't adapt to the ways of the white man.

Turkey John kept a horse trap to catch these wild horses. He had made a trap out of cottonwood poles, making a corral with a narrow gate. The gate then had two wings or pole fences that went out to guide the horses into the gate. Inside the corral he kept fresh hay that the horses could smell from outside the corral. When a horse passed through the narrow gate, he would push against the sides slightly. This would cause a pole gate to fall down behind him and trap him in the corral. It was a trick Turkey John had learned from the Indians. So healways had a good horse to break and ride. If it was one of the stolen mares, he would return it to the farmer from which it was stolen. This he would know by the brand she wore.

Turkey John left the horse in the corral until it understood that every bite it ate and every drop of water it drank came from him. The horse would begin to accept Turkey John as his friend instead of his enemy. Indians didn't rough break their horses; they gentle broke them. This produced a much more noble animal.

Christmas morning finally came. When Daddy opened the door to the old King heater to build the morning fire, three boys who usually came down about the third call after the house was warm bounded down the stairs. We had awoke before daylight and were just waiting for someone to stir downstairs so we could begin our Christmas celebration.

Instead of stockings hung, our family tradition was to place a large bowl or pan in a special place under the tree. Each kid had his own pan. The pans were full of treats and small gifts. Then there was that special-marked gift all wrapped in Christmas paper. If the paper was the same as had been used last year, no one thought a thing about it. Our family didn't throw anything away. Somehow it was supposed to help us win the war.

Dick and I were soon in the construction business that morning, with our wind-up rubber-track tractor. Emily got her doll that would cry when you turned her over and would shut her eyes when you lay her on her back. Joe was busy trying to crank his airplane motor. It had to have a special mixture of ether and alcohol, and the plug had to be heated by a battery.

Christmas breakfast was a tradition at our house. After everyone had received their gifts and the mess was all cleaned up, we sat down to a breakfast of home-cured ham, eggs, hot biscuits, and sorghum molasses. Mama always managed to have the home-cured ham, even if she had to trim it out of meat given to her by someone in the community to make lye soap from, and only fat of the meat was used to make soap. Mama was the lye-soap maker for the community and made the soap in exchange for half of it.

Chapter VI

SNOWBALL THE HERO

Tuesday, January 2, came before I was ready for it. I wasn't ready to return to school. We had been off two weeks, and during that time I had caught eight possums from Teague's woods. I had taken Snowball hunting twice. He was still too young to know what it was all about, but enjoyed barking at a squirrel when I would shoot one and field dress it.

We boys had spent many good hours in our cabin clubhouse with a good warm fire in the heater. We had even acquired two army cots to sit on and to sleep on, if we ever got brave enough to stay all night there. The cabin was just a couple hundred yards south of the cemetery, and though Harry and Fonze talked very brave, no one ventured to stay all night there. Daddy said that dead people in the cemetery can't hurt you. And I knew he was right, but they could sure make one hurt himself, running through the woods and fences scared half to death. Sometimes we would stay late in the afternoon before we went home, and we sure didn't take time to check any possum hollows on our way out to the road.

I was somewhat embarrassed about returning to school and facing Flo. She was the name I had drawn for the Christmas gift exchange in our classroom. I had bought her a nice necklace. But it didn't come in a box, so I had used a soup mix box which was about the right size to wrap it in. I had marked through the names on the box but didn't have any way to paint them out. I had wrapped it in real nice Christmas paper, with pictures of reindeer on it, and I put a colorful ribbon and bow on it. But when her name was called and she began to unwrap her gift, she had thrown it on the floor saying, "I don't want any old soup." I wanted to crawl under the seats. Her mother picked up the package and found the necklace inside. Then Flo was embarrassed, but she never spoke to me all evening, and I was too embarrassed to try to speak to her.

January at our school was not much fun. It was too cold and bad to play a good cat's eye marble game or plug tops in the schoolyard. Although, we could play a game of legging to a line with marbles in the old gym. I did get to go outside some, as I volunteered to go out to the school woodpile and bring in wood for the old big round heater in the center of our room. When the janitor got behind on those cold days, our fire would burn down, and it would get cold in our room. If the room got too cold, our teacher would let us all come up around the fire to get warm.

Warming around the fire wasn't always such a fun thing, because during the war most all of us caught the "itch." Our parents would doctor the itch with sulfur and grease (usually hog lard). When this got warm, around the fire, it smelled real bad. No one said anything though, because at one time or another we all had to wear the stinking stuff.

Once when our family had the itch, a neighbor lady who had lost her husband came to visit. She seemed to always come just at meal time and get her a plate and join our family for the meal. We didn't mind, as she lived alone and didn't like to cook just for herself. On this one visit, she joined us for the meal and stopped eating to scratch her side. She said, "Besides what ails me, I think I have the itch." We kids all ducked our heads and snickered to ourselves, for we knew that she had no doubt caught the itch from us, because we had been battling it for weeks.

Daddy had heard from someone that boiled polk root would kill the itch. So he dug up a big batch of it and boiled it for a long time on the cookstove. Then he took the water and made a bath in a number-three washtub. When he washed the raw itch rash with the polk root water, it burned terribly. He jumped out of the tub and made a couple of dashes around the kitchen. Then he told my mother, "Don't put those kids in there. It will burn them alive." So we continued the sulfur and grease treatment, putting it on at night before we went to bed and having to smell that stuff all night.

We had one good snow in January, and we kids had a good snowball fight in the schoolyard, which ended in a scrap between Monroe and me. Monroe was one of the Red River bottom kids and always seemed to have a chip on his shoulder, daring someone to knock it off. He sat behind me in the classroom, and one day he reached across me and picked up my pencil. I always carved my initials on my pencil so I would know it anywhere. He put the pencil on the edge of his desk and hit the end of it with his finger. It sailed end over end across the room and struck the teacher in the back of the head. She, more startled than hurt, shrieked, "Who struck me?" She slowly turned and looked over the room. Everyone had that "not me" look on their face, even Monroe. She then looked down and saw my cedar pencil. She bent over and picked it up. Being the only kid in the room whose initials were H. W., she immediately looked at me. I must have looked guilty, for she took me into the hall and swatted me several times with her paddle. She never bothered to ask me if I did it, though I would not have told her that Monroe was the one who did it. That was the honor code that we boys kept.

I returned to my seat without a tear, although I will admit that Miss Bedwell's left hand left her impression on me. As I turned to sit down, I whispered to Monroe, "I am going to kill you when school is out." He knew I was very serious and always kept my word.

For the rest of the day I was a hard worker. I sure didn't want to upset Miss Bedwell any more than she was, for the next time would mean a trip to the superintendent's office, and he had a special-made paddle. I didn't know firsthand about it, but I had heard that Mr. Clark could lift a boy clear off the floor with that paddle. Anyway, Mr. Clark was a good friend, and I sure wouldn't have done anything to upset that. He and his son were the ones who gave me Snowball.

That day at school was a very cold day, and I was told by my parents to eat lunch at school. School lunch cost a dime, but if you could bring a quart of canned fruit or vegetables from home, you could eat for free. We had far more jars of fruit and vegetables than we did dimes, so I had taken a jar of green beans to pay for my lunch, with instructions to be sure and bring home an empty jar. Miss Alley, our school cook, always kept a box of clean jars outside the lunchroom door for that purpose.

We had stew for lunch, made from some government canned meat and from vegetables the kids had brought from home. Also, Miss Alley had made hot chocolate from some milk that some of the kids brought in. A gallon of milk also equals the cost of a lunch. (I am sure that city schools wouldn't have approved of such trading, but in the country bartering was a way of life. A man and his team of mules in the field for ten hours was equal to two field hands for ten hours in return. Two bales of good hay was equal to one bushel of corn and so forth.)

I noticed that Monroe had sat to eat his lunch with several of the river bottom boys. I figured he was trying to get all the support he could for what was to take place after school. He knew I was one to keep my word, and I had promised him a good licking as soon as school was out. It wasn't long before the whole lunchroom was buzzing about our fight. It would no doubt be a good scrap. We were both about the same size, both hard field workers, so we would be in good shape. Maybe not as good as we were during cotton-picking season in the fall, but country boys usually have enough work to do to stay pretty lean year 'round.

After a good game of "keep away" with the basketball in the little basement gym, and a quick trip to the boys toilet at the northwest corner of the schoolyard, the big bell rang "taking up books" for the afternoon classes. The big bell would not ring again until four o'clock. We would have a fifteen-minute break at two-thirty, but only the hall bells rang for that.

After recess we ended our day of study with a spell-down. We had divided the fourth grade into two teams, lined up facing each other on each side of the room. Miss Bedwell gave the first one on each team a word to spell. When you missed a word, you had to sit down. Team after team, spellers had to sit down, until finally Lizzie and I were left facing each other. I had been lucky so far and had been given easy words, but I knew when the chips were down, Lizzie would beat me. She was a real hard studier, and I never was too serious about my homework. Sure enough, just as the big bell rang, I was stumbling through "environment," and going only by the way I pronounced it. I left out the "n." So Lizzie Dougan and her team would win if she could spell the word. She did very quickly, and Miss Bedwell dismissed the class. Monroe had inched his way up close to the door, and as soon as the teacher said, "Dismissed," he bolted for the door. By the time I cleared off my desk and got my fruit jar to take home, Monroe was far ahead of me. I was outside just in time to see him clear the school stiles and gallop away toward Red River bottom on "old Big Gray."

Monroe missed the next couple of days, which was not unusual for farm boys. They just brought a note from home saying they were working cattle or cutting cornstalks or something. By the time Monroe returned to school, I had cooled down some and felt perhaps I had already got my satisfaction when I and all the class had watched him clear the stiles and gallop away on his horse. But I was sure it would be only a matter of time before we would have to square off and settle our differences.

Each afternoon, as soon as school was out, I would rush home, change clothes, and head for

Teague's woods. My Horseshoe Lake possum bait was still working, and I got one or two possums each day. It was a good year for fur, because the cold weather had made the fur very prime, and Sears continued to pay top prices for it. But I had not shipped another possum that paid like the black one did.

Daddy had noticed a sharp fall off in the number of eggs we were getting each day from our hens. He suspected that Snowball had become a "suck-egg dog." I knew that couldn't be, for Snowball was too good of a dog for that. Daddy had a system where he kept twelve of his best hens each year and added to them twelve pullets which he handpicked and raised from the spring chicks. These pullets always laid eggs through the first winter, while the older hens molted during the late fall and would not lay eggs for about three months after they had lost their feathers. So Daddy always knew about how many eggs we should get each day.

On my own, I spent Saturday watching the henhouse and all the hens. It paid off, because one hen came out of the weeds behind the peach orchard cackling and I soon located her nest with eleven eggs in it. Also, a hen came out from under the corncrib, cackling, and I located a nest with twenty-eight eggs in it. This meant that about three hens were laying there. Because the weather had remained cold, all the eggs would still be good. Daddy was satisfied that these four hens would account for the loss of eggs that he had worried about. Snowball still had his clean record and was not a "suck-egg dog."

January passed without much to remember, but February was different. There was always Groundhog Day, Valentine Day, and the presidents' birthdays. Valentine Day was a big day in the fourth grade. Previously, it was taking a fistful of valentines to school and bringing home an equal amount. But in the fourth grade, boys began to notice that girls were different, and that one particular girl was even more different from all the rest. So a special valentine was purchased for her that was larger and different from all those valentines you bought in a package of twenty-five or fifty.

Though girls picked out their special boy, it just wasn't accepted for her to come right out and say who it was, unless it was to her closest girl-friend. So she never gave a special valentine to a boy. If any girl ever thought of me as special, she didn't say so, and I never got a special valentine card in the fourth grade.

The Saturday following Valentine Day had been set as garden clean-up day, because Mr. Bud Jones was to come Monday and break our garden with his team of horses and a turning plow. This was a yearly tradition. This year the garden was to be broken toward the middle. This was to keep from leaving a low area in the middle of the garden. It was much easier to break the soil outward, as you can start breaking all around the outside next to the fence and work toward the middle, but this turned the soil outward and always left a deep furrow down the middle of the garden to hold water when it rained.

That Saturday, our whole family was in the garden pulling and piling stalks to burn, cleaning bean poles and taking them down for a new season of Kentucky Wonder beans, and cleaning the vines from the fence for a new crop of speckled butter beans. Daddy took his pruning shears and pruned the grapevines in the south fence to ready them for a new growth. It was the new growth that produced the new crop of grapes, which Mama used to make grape jam.

About mid-morning we were all hard at work when Snowball began to bark excitedly on the east porch of the house. This was away from the garden where we could not see what he was upset about. Daddy, annoyed at the barking, yelled, "Hank, go see what is the matter with that frazzling dog." I made a dash to the east side of the house and found Snowball with his front feet upon the window screen, barking like crazy. When I got around to where I could see what he was seeing, I could see fire inside of our kitchen. I yelled, "Fire!" as loud as I could.

Joe was there by the time I got to the back door, which was on the north side of the house toward the garden. Actually, the garden was between our house and the schoolyard. Joe grabbed the water bucket that sat on the washstand beside the back door. When he entered the kitchen, he threw the water on the burning wallpaper and wall above the coal-oil cookstove. Another bucket of water was on the cook table in the kitchen, and I grabbed that and did the same. Joe grabbed the coal-oil jug that supplied the oil for the stove, and using much care, I turned the wick down on the burner that was out of control. Joe grabbed the bucket of water Mama had drawn from the well, wet a towel in it, and wrapped his hand. He took the pot of beans that had boiled over and started the fire off the stove. With the fire now almost out, Joe and I carried the stove out into the yard. Daddy made a proclamation, "I never want that thing back in my house," and it never was. Until I left home after Daddy was dead and gone, the coal-oil stove remained stored in the barn. Daddy never liked the thing anyway. He said everything that was cooked on it always tasted like coal oil. I would agree that the biscuits did, but it sure simplified the wood-cutting chores. Daddy had even invented a coal-oil burner for the old King heater, and it worked very good. My half-brother, Clyde Whitworth, filled up our kerosene barrel once a month, and that sure was easier than cutting and splitting wood.

Daddy called Snowball and gave him a pat on the head and said, "Pup, you sure saved our house today." Never again was Snowball referred to as a "suck-egg dog." I even saw Daddy saving special bones from the dinner table for Snowball. He would leave a little meat on them and take them out personally and give to the dog. Snowball was not only a good hunting dog, but he was now the animal that saved our house from burning. Now everyone could see why he meant so much to me and to the whole family.

Time was soon coming when Snowball would follow Turkey John home and become his dog. But at the present he belonged to me, and I was very proud to own such a dog.

Chapter VII

THE HAINTED BARN

February is a good month for rabbit hunting. Any month with an "r" in it is a rabbit month. May and June are rabbit nesting months. You don't hunt rabbits during that time so they can have and raise their young. Then July and August are the months that rabbits are apt to have parasites and diseases, so one doesn't kill them for food during that time. But because one pair of rabbits may raise from eight to twenty young in one season, they are always plentiful.

A "Norther" (cold wind from the north) had blown in and brought us about six inches of snow, so Dick and I took Snowball and my little single-shot .22 rifle to Hall's meadow north of the school-house to kill a rabbit. We weren't even inside of the fence yet when Snowball jumped a cottontail. The rabbit tried to run in the snow but could not, so he dove under the snow and burrowed about ten feet before he stopped to hide. I spoke to Snowball, and he froze at the hole in the snow where the rabbit went in. He watched with keen eyes for any move-ment under the snow. Now most men won't let their dogs run a rabbit, for fear they will run rabbits when you want them to tree a squirrel or possum. But Snowball was a smart dog, and he knew what I wanted him to hunt.

When Dick and I arrived at the burrow, we quickly determined by the ridge on the snow that the rabbit was about ten feet north of where he entered it. We decided to try to catch him with our hands rather than waste a rifle shell. I carefully laid the rifle down in a clump of tall dried grass, and we both got on our knees on each side of where we thought the rabbit was. With both hands we made our move and luckily pinned the rabbit down beneath the snow. I moved my left hand into the snow and took hold of his back feet and lifted him out. With a short chop behind the ears with the butt of my right hand, I snapped his neck. Then with my barlow knife I field dressed him, giving Snowball the heart and liver. I then packed the rabbit full of snow to quickly cool him out. With my knife I opened a hole beneath the large tendon above his back foot, slipped a short stick through the hole, and made an easy handle to carry the rabbit by. I picked up my rifle and instructed Snowball to "go get him," and away he ran looking for another rabbit.

Within thirty minutes we had three rabbits—one Snowball had caught outright, and two we had caught by hand in the snow. Though we had wrapped our feet with tow sacks, we were beginning to feel the cold through our shoes. We decided it was time to head home. We came to a tight five-wire fence. I laid my rifle and the rabbits on the other side of the fence, taking care not to get my gun barrel in the snow. A gun shot with snow in the barrel will blow up the barrel. I sure didn't want my little rifle to become a "sawed off" like Joe's shotgun, so I was very careful not to ever get mud or snow in the barrel. I took hold of the top barbed wire, next to a post, to step up on the first wire. I had planned to walk up the wire like a ladder, holding onto the fence post, then over and down the other side the same way. You can't slip through a tight new five-wire fence like you can an older four-wire fence. But when I pulled myself up onto the bottom wire, the fence staple pulled out of the post that held the top wire and hit me in the right eye. I could not see out of that eye at all and just knew I would be blind in it for life.

Daddy always said that "experience is the best teacher," and I can tell you right off that I never tried to climb a fence that way ever again. In about three days I began to be able to tell which side of the room had the window in it, but it took years to regain my complete sight in that eye. To this day I have a scar right on my eyeball. I never told my parents about the accident, though I know now I should have.

Daddy was real proud of us for bringing home wild meat. One rabbit was young enough to fry, and we had him for supper. The other two would have to be parboiled before they could be fried or made into rabbit stew. Daddy was also proud of us that we never had to use any rifle shells, which were very hard to come by during the war. Even if you could find them to buy, we didn't have any spare money with which to purchase them.

All week in school, stories were told about an old "hainted" barn about one-half mile north of town on the Blue River road. They told of several seeing a light in the barn at night that would raise up out of the woods, pass through the loft, then disappear down into a barn stall. It had been over twenty years since the house burned and old Mr. Salter had died in the fire. His wife and son (who they said wasn't right in his head) had left home about a year before the fire and had not been heard from since. When they tried to locate them for Mr. Salter's funeral, the wife had died and no one knew what had happened to Billy Salter, the boy. The local folks believe that the "haint" was old man Salter returning, looking for his family.

Several of us boys were talking about the barn and the stories told during our recess time. As boys will, we dared each other to go to the barn that night and see for ourselves. "Anyone who won't take a dare, will kill a hog and eat the hair, and throw the meat away." So we all agreed to meet at the corner of the Smith-Lee road and the Blue River road at six o'clock.

After school we did all our chores. Then after supper we told Daddy we were going possum hunting. He instructed us to bring him a young possum if we caught one, but we were not to take our gun because guns are too dangerous in the woods at night. Knowing that we had to have a light, I took my carbide light. I had bought it with cotton-picking money in the fall. I had a half-pint whiskey bottle full of carbide that I had gotten from Mr. Tom Smith when we were working for him. He used carbide to light his house. He had the only gas-lighted house in our county. He bought carbide by the one-hundred-pound bags, so he didn't mind giving me a bottle full. Other boys in our town and all the coon hunters could buy it by the pound can at the store for twenty-five cents a can. But I didn't have the two bits to buy a can. I also had a half-pint bottle of water in the other hip pocket for the light. When one filled the water reservoir at the top of the light and the carbide pot at the bottom, the water would slowly drip on the carbide to make gas that made the light burn. There was a flint in the reflector to light it by. One thing a boy would practice on was cupping his hand over the reflector to catch lots of gas and with one movement strike the flint while removing the hand. This would make a loud pop, and the louder the pop, the better you were at the skill of popping the light.

By the time Dick and I got to the road crossing where we were to meet the other boys, all were there except Bobby Lee. Harry, Fonze, and Jerry were there, but Bobby Lee never came. We figured he had a tough time getting permission from his mom and step-dad. We knew how terribly strict his step-dad was on him. So here we were, the guys who weren't brave enough to stay all night in the cabin we built because it was close to the grave-yard, now going to check on a "hainted" barn.

The sun had gone down, and it would be dark very soon. The wind was very cold out of the north. We walked briskly the half mile north to the barn, partly because our nerves were pushing us and partly because we were cold. We could still see some by the time we got to the barn, and in a tight group we walked through the hall of the barn, with eyes focusing on every dark shadow.

A big gray barn cat ran out of a cow stall, and we five boys bolted for the outside. Harry, who professed to be the bravest, was the first one out of the hall door and through the lot gate. Fonze, not bothering to go out of his way to go through the gate, half jumped and half clawed his way over the lot fence. We were all outside the lot when it dawned on us that it was just a cat. After we had a good laugh at each other, we made our way back to the barn. Strange though it was, there was a fire pit in the middle of the hall of the barn, lined with stones. Someone had been cooking there on an open fire. Haints don't cook; leastwise, I never heard of one doing it. We also found something strange in one of the cattle stalls. It was kind of an igloo made of bales of hay. They were stacked four high to form a small room. Some boards had been laid across the top, and more hay was laid across the top to form a roof. There was a small crawl space to enter and lots of loose hay inside to make a place to sleep. Now I sure never heard of a "haint" sleeping, nor one building an igloo out of hay. But who was staying here, and where was he now?

We boys were discussing all the possibilities of perhaps an escaped convict, someone who had been bitten by a mad dog and now had hydrophobia, a wild man, and several other undesirable folks, when we saw a light coming through the woods northwest of the barn. It was swinging back and forth, back and forth, as it moved slowly closer to us through the woods. This time we were all scared half out of our wits, even too scared to run, until Snowball began to growl a low, disturbing kind of growl. Then we all, as if on signal, bolted toward the lot gate. We ran over a little rise south of the barn and fell into a deep gully. There we lay for some time. Finally, I eased up the bank of the gully and peeped over the rise. The light was a coal-oil lantern which was now hanging in the hall of the barn. Someone was busy building a fire in the cooking pit. With an old pot he had no doubt salvaged from the dump below the barn, he put what looked like a rabbit on the fire to boil.

The man had on funny-looking clothes.

They were some kind of hospital clothes but were all tattered and torn. My guess was that this was Billy Salter, who had escaped from a mental hospital and had come home, but found no home. His dad and mom were dead. The county had taken over the property and sold it to Bill Williams for back taxes. The house had burned, and nothing was left but the old big barn and it was in poor repair. Bill still stored some hay in it but wouldn't let his cows spend the night in it for fear the wind might blow it down on them. We boys agreed we would not tell a soul that the "haint" was Billy Salter. He seemed to be making it OK, and we, like most all country people, believe in leaving folks alone.

After solving the "haint" mystery, we made our way down the gully into E. P. Hall's branch west of the big barn. We hadn't gone very far before Snowball barked on a tree. We lit our carbide lights with several good pops and quickly spotted a pair of eyes looking back at us from up a persimmon tree. It was a possum, and we began to climb the tree to kick him out. When the possum hit the ground, Snowball was right on top of him, and the possum went into his playing dead act, which we called "sulling."

I called the dog off, and Harry quickly broke the possum's neck. This method of killing a possum was quick and painless to the possum but also did not harm the pelt. With sharp knives in every boy's pocket, it was no time before we had the possum skinned and were on our way to find another. A good dog would already be hunting for another, but Snowball was a young dog and not yet trained to do that. But with a "sick 'em" signal from me, he raced off through the woods, and in five minutes had a second possum up a tree.

That night we caught five possums before we turned for home. Harry said that his stretching boards were empty because his dad had shipped his hides that day, so he took the hides home and said that he would split the money with all of us. Dick and I had the longest way to go, so we headed home, cutting southwest across Hall's pasture, then across Bill Williams' pasture to the Baptist church house, then home. It was about ten o'clock when we got into bed. We were feeling pretty proud that we had solved the "hainted barn" mystery and even caught five possums. Snowball had done himself quite well in front of all our friends. The real joy of the evening, though, was our agreement to keep a secret about Billy Salter.

Chapter VIII

APRIL FOOL'S DAY

March had come in on a stiff wind from the south. The Canadian geese and ducks used this northbound wind to blow them back to their summer nesting and feeding grounds on the Canadian lakes. We boys' minds were on kites. Each boy had his own favorite design and building material. I liked small round bamboo cane from Blue River bottom for my sticks and newspaper for my cover. I always made the diamond-shaped kite and used flour paste to put the cover on with.

Saturday morning was to be kite-flying day. We were to meet at the west end of the schoolyard near the ball diamond. Then after we flew our kites, we were to choose sides and play our first softball game of the season. Dick and I had worked all week on our kite. The bridle setting and the length of the tail had to be just right. We had made ours a little bigger than usual, to catch all the wind we could. Yet, I knew that if the wind was too high, my cotton string just would not hold it. I had been saving string for a couple of years. Every time we bought something or received a package in the mail, it would be wrapped and tied with cotton string. I had saved these pieces and tied them all together and rolled them on my kite spool. Daddy had made my kite-flying spool for me. It had a handle on it and a crank on one side for winding in the kite string. Dick and I had tested our kite several times and knew it would fly without making power dives in the wind gusts. We had the bridle setting just right, and the weight of the tail was sufficient to hold it upright. Joe had made a box kite and covered it with model-airplane tissue paper. It was a beautiful kite. I had never tried to make one of those, mainly because I didn't understand just what made it fly.

Saturday came and by the time we had finished our Saturday morning gardening chores, boys had already begun to gather in the schoolyard. Joe, Dick, and I were soon among the rest. There was a good stiff wind right out of the south, so we soon had our kites up with the rest of the kites. Joe's box flew silent and steady. It was by far the best-looking kite in the air. My kite kept taking string and rising until it was just a small speck in the sky. I was afraid my knotted string might break, taking that much pull.

Boys began to send messages up to their kite by writing them on a small piece of paper and putting it around their kite string in a cone shape. They stuck it together with spit. When the wind

80

caught the cone-shaped paper, it would begin to move along the string up toward the kite. I couldn't do that because my string was full of knots, being made of short pieces of string all tied together. My kite was up higher than the rest, so no one said anything about my knotted string.

After about an hour of kite flying, someone yelled, "I get to play first base," and the kites began to be rolled in. My kite was the first one down, even though it was up the highest, because of the neat crank spool my daddy had made me. Joe didn't take his box down but just tied it up to a post on the schoolyard fence on the south side of the yard. It actually flew out over the ball field but too high to ever be hit with a batted ball. Joe didn't play ball with us but returned home. I knew he had something on his mind, and I wondered just what it might be.

We didn't have enough boys for two teams, so we decided to play work-up. We had to have four batters in case three got on base, the fourth would knock them in. But that left us short one to cover all the positions on the field. We decided that the fourth batter would do the hind-catching until that time when the first three batters were on base, then the right fielder would come in and catch. Ed Reed and I were the only two who could throw a windmill pitch, so we would do all the pitching and exchange when it was time for the pitcher to bat. When a batter made an out, he would then go to right field, and everyone else would rotate except the pitcher. I am sure all this would be hard to write in a rule book, but it worked for us.

This being my first game of the season, I was glad when it came my time to bat. My arm was getting heavier by the pitch. I hadn't been thinking much about softball, so I hadn't been working out with my rubber ball against the well house. I had bought a rubber ball the size and weight of a softball to pitch at a target on the side of the well house. It being rubber, it would bounce back to me each time I pitched it.

When it was my time at bat, Ed Reed, who like myself was not in pitching form, threw me a fat one right across the plate about knee high. I knocked it to short right for a base hit. I stole second following the next pitch, then Jerry hit a double and I came home. Jerry, Harry, and I held bats until everyone was getting tired, then from all the way across our little town we heard Donnie's mother call, "Buddie, dinner is ready." No doubt she had the strongest voice I had ever heard. Anyway, this broke up the game, and everyone headed home.

When I got home, Joe had the biggest kite I had ever seen almost made. He was putting paper on it. It was wider than I was tall and higher than Joe when he stood up. He had borrowed Daddy's Red River trout-line cord, which was almost as big around as a pencil. It was about three hundred yards long. He had torn up one of Mama's old sheet blankets to use as a tail for the kite.

After he glued the paper on with airplane glue and bridled the kite, he was ready to launch it. Mama said that dinner was ready and that we could go after we had eaten. Leo Clark and Billy Wayne Smith had come over to help Joe build the kite, so they joined us for dinner. We had chicken and dumplings and Mama's canned green beans, and she had baked a chocolate pie for dessert. After we had finished eating, we headed back to the school-yard to launch the big kite.

The box kite was still flying, and Joe decided we had better take it down in fear they would get tangled up. Then with a couple of adjustments to the bridle, the big kite was soon in the air. It took two of the teenage boys to hold the cord, and even then they had to dig their heels into the dirt to keep from being drug by it. Joe had on a leather glove to keep the cord from burning his hand as he let out more cord. Finally, all of the cord was out. At three hundred yards high it didn't look any bigger than a regular kite, but all three of the teen boys were holding on to the cord for dear life. Up there where the big kite was, the wind was much stronger. Finally the cord broke and we all stood without a word, watching the great kite blow northward until it went out of sight across E. P. Hall's woods.

Joe sadly rolled up Daddy's cord, and we headed home with a great tale to tell of the largest kite ever built. We would wait until tomorrow to go see if we could find the kite and the rest of Daddy's cord.

Sunday afternoon Joe and I went across Hall's farm looking for the big kite. We finally found it. It was almost to Blue River, about two miles north of the school where we were flying it. The big kite was still in one piece, hanging by a piece of the cotton cord in the top of a large cotton-wood tree. It was too high to climb up and get, so both of us pulled on the end of the cord that was laying on the ground, until we tore it down. Joe really wasn't interested in flying the big kite again. When he did something once, he turned to something new and different to try. So the fact that we destroyed the kite in pulling it down was all right with Joe. He just wanted all of Daddy's cord back. Though my daddy would probably never go fishing again, as he said he was too old, he sure did like to take care of things. It was wartime, and one couldn't buy everything he wanted, even if he had the money. We had just gone through the Great Depression where Daddy went broke selling groceries from his store, on credit, to people who were hungry and had no money.

March passed quickly, and next Friday would be April Fool's Day. The tradition for we country boys was to play hookey from school. Our school principal, Mr. Teague, had asked our town smithy to make him a special paddle out of seasoned black-locust wood, just for the occasion. He

had promised ten licks with his new board to anyone playing hookey on April Fool's Day.

Tuesday afternoon Mr. Teague left his paddle on his desk during recess. Monroe took my barlow knife from my study desk, where I had been
carving my initials on my new pencil, and slipped
into Mr. Teague's office and took a large cut out of
the black-locust paddle. Then he returned the knife
to my desk. He didn't own a knife, so he himself
wouldn't be a suspect. Soon after recess, a runner
came to each room asking for all boys who owned
a knife to report to the principal's office. One by
one he took the knives and fitted them into the cut
on his paddle, while he watched the eyes of the boy
who owned the knife. When he came to my knife,
I would have been OK, but Monroe told Jerry, and
Jerry had told me, that it was my knife. He fitted
the knife several times into the cut place. When he
had tried all the knives, he asked me, Jerry, and
Bobby Lee to remain behind while he excused all
the rest of the boys to return to their rooms. Bobby
Lee didn't know about the situation, but he was a
nervous type and could have easily looked guilty
even though he had nothing to do with it.

After about ten minutes of direct questioning
and being asked point blank, "Did you do
it?"–which all of us could answer no–we were then
dismissed to return to our room with the great mystery unsolved. But one more time my "friend"
Monroe had managed to almost get me into trouble,

and part of the anger I felt before when he used my pencil to strike Miss Bedwell in the back of the head returned. When I returned to the classroom, Monroe made sure he was very busy reading in his speller. I am sure he knew I was looking a hole through him as I returned to my seat.

After school a number of us were walking together on our way home. We were busy planning our fishing trip to Horseshoe Lake come Friday. We had heard that the fifth and sixth graders were going to Red River, and we didn't want to be with them. We were to meet at Uncle Jim Teague's barn (he was not our uncle, but everyone called him that), which is just east of the school grounds. We would leave from there as soon as the last bus had run. This was to give plenty of time for Wendell and others who rode the busses to join us if they wanted to. Some of the girls wanted to go along, but we quickly ruled that out. It would just mess up everything. For not only were we going fishing, but this was to be our first swim of the year, and who would want to mess with a bathing suit all day long?

Daddy knew that Dick and I would be going, and he didn't try to stop us. He even helped us dig a Prince Albert tobacco can full of worms, but we had to promise to bring him a good catfish. So on Friday morning we were ready to go. Teague's barn was just across the road east of our orchard. We were the first ones there. With a P.A. can filled with worms and hooks in our pocket, we were ready to go.

It was almost time for the big school bell to ring the "take up books" call when the boys from the last bus arrived. To my surprise Monroe was one of the boys arriving to go. Our number added up to exactly twelve. We had been called "the dirty dozen" by some of the town folks. We made our way through town by staying off the streets. We followed the branch to the cemetery road, then past Rice Creek on the Smith-Lee road, to the Shastid place. We went north through Mr. Shastid's field to Horseshoe Lake.

We each cut bamboo poles from the river bottom sufficient for each hook we had brought and were soon fishing. I chose an old cedar log that had fallen out into the lake. I walked the log out as far as I dared, then set out my hooks, baiting with a large worm on each one. By noon I had a fair string of fish staked out on a cotton cord that I had brought for that purpose.

Snowball had gone with us, and he was trailing a rabbit over on the bank of the river, not far from where I was fishing. It wasn't long until he jumped the rabbit, and the race was on. Even though I couldn't see dog or rabbit, I knew he was gaining from the excitement in his bark. Then I heard him bark on bay and decided I had better go see what he had. I found him at the foot of a large hickory tree that had a hollow at the bottom. I took a piece of barbed wire from an old fence nearby and made me a twist out of it. Pushing the wire up past the rabbit, who was about four feet up, I began to turn the wire around and around. I soon had his fur rolled up in the wire, and I gently began to pull until I had him down far enough to reach his hind foot with my other hand. When I pulled him out and loosened his fur from the barbed wire, I found that he was a large swamp rabbit. These rabbits are much bigger than a cottontail.

I dressed him with my barlow knife and put him on a spit over a fire I had made. Roast rabbit is mighty good when boys are on a creek bank without any lunch, and it was still too early in the spring to glean dewberries or wild grapes to satisfy one's hunger. Some of the other boys added fish to the spit, and before long we all had at least a piece of meat each.

As soon as our lunch was over, someone yelled, "Swimming time," and, "Last one in is a tar baby." The race was on. To undress was not much chore, because all we had on was a t-shirt and a pair of overalls. One flip of the gallus buckle and the overalls would fall to the ground. Then one slip of the t-shirt with one's hand catching the collar behind the neck and you were in your birthday suit. But with one dip of the big toe in the cold river water, no one was jumping in. The banks were still muddy and slick from spring rains, so I carefully made my way down to the water. When I, like the rest, decided it was too cold, I began to make my way up the slick bank. My first swim of the year would just have to wait a few weeks. Monroe slipped up behind me and rubbed a handful of cold black mud all over my back, even getting it in my hair. So now I would have to go in and wash off. That was the straw that broke the camel's back. I turned around and wrestled him down into the mud. With handfuls of mud, I rubbed his hair, face, and all over his body. We both began to slip and slide down the slippery bank until we were in the ice-cold river. I was so mad I didn't even notice how cold it was. Monroe managed to escape my grasp and began to climb up the river bank. I grabbed him by the ankle and dragged him back into the water. He went under, and each time he came up I pushed him back down. He came up coughing and spitting and yelling, "I've had enough!" I pushed him down just one more time, to say, also, that I had had enough of his jokes. They were not very funny when I came out on the brunt end of them each time.

I washed all the mud off and made my way back up the bank to my clothes and got dressed. When I got back to the lake and my fishing log, I had a good catfish on one of my hooks, but he was tangled badly around some brush. When I finally worked him free, we guessed him to weigh about five pounds. Daddy would get his good mess of catfish, after all. This one plus the five other ones I had on my stringer would make a heavy load to carry home.

By the time we walked the two miles home, the day would be about over and it would be time to do chores, so we all decided to head for home. Those who came on the bus had an extra mile or so to walk. We knew the bus driver would have instructions from the principal that no one was to ride who didn't attend school that day. We all hoped that Mr. Teague would forget the whole thing over the weekend, but we were just trying to fool ourselves on April Fool's Day.

Daddy took the job of cleaning the catfish, and we boys began the evening chores. It had been a good day, and a catfish supper would be a good finish for it. But I knew I would not stay awake long enough that night to read in my book by the light of my flashlight. I was a tired boy.

Chapter IX

RUN, JOHNNIE, RUN

I was a little late getting to school on Monday morning, as Daddy decided it was time to plant watermelons and that had to be done before we could go to school. The warning bell had already rung by the time I got to the schoolyard, and that meant I only had five minutes to get to my room and in my seat before the big bell rang to "take up books." The day always began with the singing of "America the Beautiful," the flag salute, and then a prayer (usually the Lord's Prayer). At the close of the opening exercise, a runner came to the door with a list of names of boys who were to report to the principal's office immediately.

I swallowed real big, as the names were read of all my fishing buddies, including my own name. Bobby Lee, whose name was on the list, began to fumble in his pocket and came out with a note from his mother excusing him from school Friday. He had a big grin on his face and cut his eyes over to see if I was watching. He could always talk his mother into anything, but his father was a different story. I knew better than to ask my daddy for a note, even though I had brought him a good mess of fish. Somehow, he thought a good busting now and then made a boy grow up stronger and smarter–somehow. All I ever knew it did for me was burn me on my sitting-down place.

I was tenth in line at Mr. Teague's office that day. He was left handed, and by the time he got to me, he wasn't swinging that big soap paddle very hard and he was all out of breath. I was afraid that he would put me off until afternoon and then I would be first in line, but he didn't. His ten licks weren't very hard at all, and the extra padding of the two handkerchiefs I had borrowed from Daddy's clothes drawer and slipped down inside my overalls sure did help. Even then I was glad my name wasn't Allen or Branch and that I wasn't up in the head of the line as Donnie and Jerry were. The name Whitworth is hard to spell and also hard to pronounce for some people, but it sure comes in handy sometimes.

We heard that after morning recess he called all the fifth- and sixth-grade fishermen out for their licking. They had gone to Red River and also chickened out and didn't go swimming because the water was too cold. We told them some of us had gone swimming but didn't give them the details. All the boys kinda kept the scrap between Monroe and me a secret, because they, as we, feared we would get extra licks if it got back to the principal.

It rained all week, almost day and night. Daddy said that Blue River would be coming out of its banks, so we boys talked about going to Blue on Saturday to catch some fish where the overflow water runs through the slew. There was a bridge across the slew, just before you get to the Blue River bridge. Each year during overflow time, the men of the community would fence off the slew at one end of the bridge. When the water began to go back down, the fish would be trapped by the chicken wire and would congregate along the wire trying to find a way to get back to the river. One would use gigs or dip nets made from chicken wire to catch the fish, and sometimes, if the water wasn't too cold, they would go into the water with the fish and catch them with their hands. I didn't care much for that method, as large moccasin snakes sometimes came down the slew and swam under the bridge.

Jerry had talked his grandfather into loaning us the wagon and mules, provided we would come back by the old stump field and pull some stumps to cut up into wash-pot wood. Now the wash pot sat out in the back yard and was used to heat water for washing clothes, making lye soap, making hominy, and many other things around the place. It sat up on cast-iron legs, usually placed on bricks or large rocks, and was fired with heart wood or stump wood, as they made a hotter fire.

It was a nice morning. There was a skimmer of clouds that had moved in after the sun came up, yet all the birds were happy for a nice day after all that rain. Three families of purple martins had come to stay the summer with us in our martin houses Daddy had built. A family of bluebirds had moved into the hollow post at the corner of the garden. They come every year. I often wondered if it was the same ones or a young one from last year's nest. The wrens and the cardinals had also arrived. Daddy believed that all these birds were a natural way to keep down insects that become pests during the gardening season, so he did everything he could to encourage them to come and stay with us. We also used chicken and cow manure to fertilize our garden and orchard with. Well, that was until some high-school boys stole some sulfuric acid from the school lab and poured it on old Tight-Tit to make her run. But instead of making her just run, it ate a hole through her back, and Daddy had to shoot her to keep her from suffering so. We could have dressed her and made beef roast and canned meat, but none of us would have eaten a bit of it because she had been our milk cow as long as I could remember. We dug a deep hole at the back of the orchard and buried her. We sure missed that rich milk and butter, but most of all we missed old Tight-Tit.

We boys met at Jerry's house and walked up to his grandfather's house for the wagon and team. The mules, Huldy and Jude, were in the barn lot and were no trouble to catch. We put the harness on them, and the mules automatically walked to the wagon tongue and got on the side of the tongue that they were in the habit of pulling from. Huldy was always on the left and Jude on the right. We snapped their trace chains onto the single trees that they pulled from and raised the tongue into place and hooked it onto their collars and we were off.

Beings that we would be going north right by Billy Salter's barn, I suggested that we swing around by our cabin and take one of the army cots and some pots and pans to Billy. We reasoned that if we left them in the dump near Billy's barn that he would find them and put them to use. We all agreed, so we headed the team of mules toward the cemetery and through the gate into the woods just south of the cemetery. We could get the wagon just across the creek from our log cabin, so we didn't have to carry the steel cot very far. We also took some coffee, lard, and other food stuff that we had borrowed a little at a time from our mothers' kitchens. We gave Billy our coffee pot, a skillet, and a stew pan that we ourselves had salvaged from a dump.

We were careful to stop the wagon over the hill from Billy's barn and carry the things back to the dump by traveling up the branch. None of us wanted to come face to face with someone who had escaped from an institution. We heard later that Billy had muscular dystrophy. But when I was nine years old, folks didn't know anything about that and considered it mental illness because they walked funny and couldn't talk where one could understand them. After leaving the stuff where Billy would be sure to find it, we all got back into the wagon and headed for Blue River.

Traveling by wagon and mules is very slow. Mr. Allen would have skinned us alive if we ever ran or even trotted his mules. But boys jumping in and out of the tail of the wagon, running alongside and chunking those in the wagon with clods of dirt or mudballs, made the time pass more quickly. Soon we were at the slew bridge. The water was going down, as we could tell from the watermarks on the trees and bridge. We tied the mules and wagon up to a tree across the bridge and began to unload the chicken wire and equipment that we had brought.

The water was very swift, so we tied a lariat rope across the slew, between two trees, just above the bridge. Then holding onto the rope to keep from being swept under the bridge, we pulled the chicken wire across. We nailed it to the wooden planks of the bridge and staked it down to the bottom. To do that, one had to go down under the water and push the stakes through the wire and down into the muddy bottom. This was not an easy job, and Harry and the bigger boys had to do it. In about an hour the task was finished, and we were already feeling big fish come down the slew and bump into the wire.

Soon we were catching fish in the dip nets we had built of chicken wire. These fish had come up out of the river during the overflow to feed on worms and insects that the overflow water had exposed. Then when the water started back down, they would hurry back to the river, else they would be trapped in the slew all summer. This is how Turkey John explained it to me. We strung the fish on a cord and tied them out in the water below the bridge to keep them alive until we were ready to go home.

We had caught about ten fish when A. J. Jones came riding up on a paint horse. His father raised paints and taught them to fox trot and sold them for riding horses. They were about the best in the whole country. A. J. was a teenager and was out riding the river looking for some of his dad's cows or horses that might be trapped by overflow water. He was smoking a cob pipe, and the smoke was just rolling. He got off his paint and tied him to the wheel of our wagon and joined us on the bridge. He said to me, "I'll let you smoke my pipe if you will let me use your net to catch a fish." To this I readily agreed, as I had never smoked a pipe before and was always on the lookout for a new experience.

He knocked out his pipe and packed it full of some tobacco from a cloth sack. It was labeled R.J.R., which the locals called "RUN, JOHNNIE, RUN." He pulled the strings and closed the bag, then handed me the pipe with a match to light it with. I lay on the bridge watching A. J. fish and blowing big puffs of smoke into the air and watched it float away. Now and then I cut my eyes to the other boys to see if they were watching how big I looked smoking a cob pipe. But before long the bridge began to move and the water running beneath the bridge did funny things. I was as sick as a mule, as my daddy would say, but I never in all my life saw a mule as sick as I was.

I don't remember much more about the day's fishing, only that I was sitting up on the springboard of the wagon with Jerry and he yelled, "Get up!" and ran against a stump that he had tied a chain to. The stump didn't move, but we pulled the whole rear end out of the wagon. He had tied the chain to the back axle instead of the coupling pole, and the pin broke that keeps the axle in place on the pole. In the process, I fell off the wagon and was looking up at the belly of two very excited mules. I managed to roll out from under the mules with only one footprint on my leg.

I don't know whether it was the excitement of the fall and mules and all that sobered me up or the hard work helping pick up the wagon and putting the wheels back under it, but I was no longer sick and the world quit spinning around. I decided though that that was enough RUN, JOHN-NIE, RUN to do me for the rest of my life. We loaded up the stumps that we had lost and some more that we could pull by hand and headed home.

Other than being sick, it was good day. We had Mr. Allen's wood and enough fish for almost the whole town.

Chapter X

TURKEY JOHN'S HOME

School was out the first week in May. We so looked forward to that. Now I can look back and wonder why, as we only exchanged school work for much harder work in the fields. But I guess it was the confinement of school that boys hated so. I was able to pass on to the fifth grade, even though my grades were not very good. Skipping the third grade may had seemed like a good move to the teachers and to my parents, but it sure made it hard on me. Maybe I should have told them that the reason I scored the highest on the county test was that I worked out an Ennie-Minnie-Myne-Mo system to answer all the true-and-false and multiple-choice questions. Mr. Clark was trying to keep our high school. If the enrollment went below sixty, we would have to consolidate with another school, so he was making sure that each grade had enough kids in it to keep up that much enrollment. That is mostly why they had Duggie, Kenneth, Liz, and me skip from the second to the fourth. The second was a large class, and the third only had six in it. We would make it at least ten going into the fourth grade. We lost our high school anyway, for people kept moving away to find work in the defense plants. So it really didn't help any for me to skip the third grade.

I got a job right off hoeing Hollis McIntire's corn. It was ten hours a day for four dollars, which was pretty good pay for a nine-year-old. Very few my age would the farmers hire, but they knew my daddy had taught me how to work. I could hoe from either the left or right side, which I used when I got tired doing it one way. I made better money picking cotton in the fall, but you are paid for the pounds you pick rather than the hours that you work. We worked six days a week, only leaving Sundays off. No one worked on Sunday where I came from. You would be classified a heathen if you did, and no one wanted to be called that, even though not many folks in our town went to church, especially since the Mission burned and the Baptist and Methodist had no preacher. The only church we had was summer tent or brush-arbor meetings, where a preacher would come through the country holding meetings. Also, each summer the Cherokees would camp over on Cherokee Lake northwest of town and have a big brush-arbor meeting. This is something they began during the Civil War when in the summertime the Union soldiers would come down into Oklahoma Territory from Fort Scott, up in Kansas, and take all their young braves and draft them into the Union army. So the Cherokees would spend the summer down in the Choctaw territory. Then each summer they came back kinda as a summer camp or outing and stayed about four weeks.

On Sunday, after our family was finished with our family worship time, we boys were free to play or do whatever we wanted to, as long as it wasn't considered "working on Sunday." Fishing and hunting were considered work, because you did it for the meat, and even to this day, I still can't fish or hunt on Sunday, even though it would be strictly recreational. One just doesn't get away from his teachings. So, on this second Sunday of May, we boys decided to bumble-bee fight. Off we went to recruit some fellow warriors to help us fight. We knew of a bumble-bee nest in the ground at the east end of the school gym that we had found during school days.

We were able to recruit about eight boys, and we each made a cedar-shingle paddle from shingles we borrowed from the roof of Grannie Burns' old barn. Each boy had his favorite design. I always liked to drill several holes in my paddle with my barlow knife so that the paddle wouldn't blow the bees away but would pull them to one of the holes which wasn't big enough for a bee to go through. Usually one swat and he was a dead bee. Our fight plan was to encircle the bee hole about ten yards out and move slowly in toward it, swatting each warrior bee that attacked. One had to keep a keen eye for bees returning from gathering nectar, because they could attack from the rear. If they were heavy loaded with pollen and nectar, they wouldn't bother you but would go straight to the hole. Unlike honey bees, which build their hive in hollow trees or boxes people make especially for them, the bumble bees hive in the ground. They dig out chambers and fill them with honey sacks and other chambers with the same kind of sacks with their young grubs in them.

In about twenty minutes we had fought our way in over the hole, then we killed each single bee as he came out of the hole and rose to fly. It takes some time for a bumble bee to get airborne, but after he gets up he can fly at great speed. If you should miss one with your paddle and he hits you between the eyes (their favorite spot), you surely feel the pop, then the sting will swell both eyes shut in just a few minutes. Bumble-bee sting is far worse than honey bee or yellow jacket.

Finally the bees quit coming out, and we knew we had them licked. We took a shovel that we had brought for that purpose and carefully dug into the chambers of honey pods. Each boy ate his fill of the honey. One has to be careful not to eat too much, for it will make you sweet sick. It is much richer than honey-bee honey. Bobby Lee mentioned a bumble-bee hive in his back pasture. Feeling good about our victory, we were ready to take on another hive, so we headed that way. What

Bobby Lee didn't tell us was that the bumble bees had dug their hole under a pair of half-buried bed springs.

On one side of the bed springs was a ditch and some trees and brush, so we couldn't make a circle around them. We decided our best hope was to form a line and just attack from the front. We had the boys on each end to face outward to kill the bees that went around through the woods and attacked us from the flanks. Our plan worked pretty good until I was hit from the rear by a bee returning to the hive. He stuck in the hair of my head and began to buzz like crazy. I broke ranks, running and swatting at my head like a crazy person, but I could not dislodge the bee. I ran toward the road and jumped the fence, and at that same time Fonze's little brother was coming down the road with ten pounds of ice on a pair of ice hooks. He had bought it at Land's store and was taking it to his mother to use for ice tea for dinner. To my surprise and his, the bee quit me and got in his hair. Ice went one way, tongs went another, and Cal ran screaming toward home. I felt sorry for him, but not enough to keep from laughing.

Up on the bluff on the other side of the fence, the whole bee-fighting army was laughing like crazy. Fonze was the first one to jump the fence and began trying to find the ice hooks and pick up the dirty ice. We all helped clean off the ice with our hands and shirt sleeves the best we could, and Fonze headed home figuring he would be in trouble with his dad when he got there. We all decided that the bed-springs bees would have to wait until next Sunday, and we headed home, also. For some reason Fonze's little brother never did like me after that. It was like he thought I did it on purpose or something. I don't think he ever did get stung.

May passed rather quickly, and to a nine-year-old that means without many different things happening. On rainy days when we couldn't work in the fields, there was always garden to gather or hoe. Daddy didn't have the same rules that the local farmers had about hoeing in the rain or in muddy fields. If it was really raining too hard, one could always clean out the chicken house or shell corn in the crib or something.

Along the last of May I got a job for Watson Seed Company pulling tassels out of corn grown for seed. They would have a farmer plant four rows of one kind of corn (which we called female) and two rows of another kind of corn (which we called male). We kept the tassels pulled out of the female corn, and they would be pollinated by the male corn. The four rows were then gathered in the fall and sold for hybrid seed corn. The farmer could use the other corn to feed his stock, or the seed company would buy it for next year's crop. The job paid five dollars per day, and one rode on big machines that carried you up above the corn so you could reach the tassels in the tall river-bottom corn. There was always good long breaks every couple hours and usually a swim in the river at lunch time.

The last Sunday in May, Joe, Dick, and I rode our bikes to Red River to get Snowball. He had followed Turkey John home after he had come to visit us. Snowball took a liking to Turkey John as did all other animals. He called Snowball "Bobang." I never knew if this name had a meaning in Cherokee or if he just didn't like the name I had given him.

Turkey John lived on what was called the beach, which was a stretch of sandy land between the Bayou and Red River. Actually, he lived right on the bank of the river but was supposed to watch the Hauk brothers' cattle which was summer grazing that land. Mostly Turkey John fished, hunted, and broke wild horses. He sold enough fish to buy what staple food he needed and yeast for the beer he made for himself, but other than that he didn't need much money.

That Sunday, John had been out in his cottonwood boat running his lines and nets. I guess he didn't care if someone called him a heathen. He wouldn't know what that meant anyway. Bobang was standing right in front of the boat, barking like crazy at every turtle or snake he saw, and especially when he saw us standing on the bank of the river. They had several nice catfish and a sturgeon he had taken from his lines, and several big blue buffalo fish he had taken out of the nets. He put them all in a live box that floated in the edge of the river. It had several compartments in it, one for catfish, one for buffalo, etc.

Turkey John dressed a nice buffalo fish for our dinner and fried him a golden grown in his skillet. After we ate, we talked a while, and Turkey John told us of a new paint horse he had trapped down the river. He was breaking her to ride. It was too far down there for us to go see, but when we came again, he would show her to us.

John lived in a dugout in the sand bank of the river. There were steps leading down into the one-room house. He had cut logs and laid them across the dugout to hold up the roof, then he had piled dirt on the top to keep out the rain. There was a canvas lean-to built out over the steps and doorway to keep it from raining in the doorway and running under the door. Inside was a bed he had made of wooden poles on blocks of wood and a mattress of straw and duck and goose feathers from his winter game he had trapped or shot.

On the other side of the room was a wooden table with a kerosene lantern on it and some tin plates and cups. There was a little fireplace in the end, dug back into the bank and lined with rocks, with the chimney being just a hole dug up through the dirt to the top. This was for indoor cooking when it was bad outside and some added heat in the winter when one came in chilled. Actually the temperature in the dugout stayed about the same in summer and winter. The fireplace flue would produce some air flow as the air would come under the door and go up the chimney. Turkey John said now and then a ground squirrel or a pack rat would come down the flue and mess with things on his table. One time a rattlesnake came in that way, but Turkey John killed him.

There were no books or papers about, as Turkey John could just barely read or write. Mama wrote him a letter now and then, but he never answered her back. I doubt if he could write enough to write a letter. His use of the English language was mixed with about half Cherokee and half English. He was almost bald headed, which he inherited from the white man, but he had no beard on his face, a trait he had gotten from the Indians. All summer he wore only a pair of cutoff pants, no shirt, and no shoes. He did wear a big felt hat that was creased in the middle of the crown like an old-time cowboy. His hat would have one large turkey feather in it. I never knew if he wore it because folks called him turkey or if it had some Indian meaning. Some things a boy just doesn't ask.

Out beside the dugout was a table made with two cottonwood planks nailed to the top of a big cottonwood stump. This served as a stand-up eating table and a cook table. Most of his cooking was done over an open fire in a fire pit he had made in the ground and lined with stones. Also, there was a lean-to of canvas and a couple of chairs for sitting, made of bent willow which grew plentiful up and down the river bank.

Turkey John's dish washer was a long willow

pole with a cotton cord tied to the end of it. He would string his plates, cups, skillet, etc., on the cord, through a hole in the outer edge or handle. Then he would stake them out into the river by sticking the end of the pole in the sand bank. This let the swift water and the rolling sand clean them as clean as if they had been scoured with a soap pad. He said, "Simple men have simple ways," but his grin let me know that he felt like that was pretty smart. I did, also.

It was soon time to head home. I put a string on Snowball for fear he might just decide to stay, and by the way he looked over his shoulder as we rode away, I believe he would have. John sent Daddy a nice channel catfish, which we tied onto Joe's handlebars. So with Dick and I on the Hawthorne and Snowball in tow on a string and Joe on his Schwinn, we headed home. As we rode away, Turkey John said, "You boys come back and spend a week with me in July when the crops are all laid by, and we will do some fishing."

It was about three miles home and most of the way uphill out of the river bottom, so we were plenty tired when we got home. Daddy cleaned the fish while we boys did the chores, and after a good fish supper we turned in early. The next day would be a ten-hour day for Joe and me in the cornfield. My last thought was Turkey John's invitation to come back in July and spend a week. I could learn more about the wild in a week with him than I could in a lifetime in school or by myself in the woods.

Chapter XI

KILLED THE SACRED BIRD

June turns hot in southern Oklahoma. The temperature often climbs above one hundred degrees and just stays there for days. Work in the cornfields was about all over now, but next we would begin hoeing peanuts and chopping cotton (it was called chopping because you had to thin the plants to hoe-width apart, as well as hoe out the grass). Farmers bailing hay always needed workers around the hay presses and for hauling it into the barns, but they only paid half-wages to a nine-year-old. Then we would have several peach trees ripen in June, and spare time was used in picking and peeling peaches for Mama to can. Daddy would often sell peaches by the bushel. Peaches for ourselves could be shaken out of the tree and picked up off the ground, but peaches to sell had to be hand picked and placed carefully in the basket. I doubt that the buyer could tell the difference, but my daddy would not sell anyone bruised fruit. He was just that way.

Saturday was a day off from work. We had a June shower that stopped the hay work for a few days, and the fields were all too wet to hoe. Daddy decided it would be a good day to can the Indian peaches that grew along the path next to the garden. There were two trees of these, so we shook off about two bushels and picked them up. That path led to our outhouse, which was at the back of our orchard. Boy, was it a long way down that path on a cold winter night.

Leo Clark had come over to buddy with Joe, and Joe, being the Tom Sawyer that he was, talked Leo into helping us peel a tub full of peaches. We drew a couple of buckets of cold water from the well to pour over the tub of peaches to wash them. As a boy would pick up a peach, somehow water got slung onto another boy, and the water flipping began. That is, until Daddy reminded us that the sooner we finished the tub of peaches, the sooner we could go play. He was always careful to teach us the reason for work, rather than just make us do it, although there were times when he would say, "Just because I told you to do it," if you pressed him a little as to why.

After an hour or so, the peaches were peeled, and we were all out in the yard doing a little knife plugging. Leo, in fun, made out like he was going to plug my toe with the butcher knife he had been using peeling peaches. I yelled, "You had better not." He did it again, and this time the knife slipped, or he was sure that he could miss my toes. Either way, he cut off the next to the smallest toe on my right foot. It was barely hanging on my foot by some skin on one side. I screamed, and Mom came running. My foot was bleeding terrible. Mom made me sit with my foot in a pan of kerosene until the bleeding stopped, then Daddy put the toe back in place and taped it on with a lot of tape after he poured a bunch of rubbing alcohol on it. We lived about twenty-five miles from the nearest doctor and had no way to get there even if we had the money to pay a doctor bill. I had to wear that tape for about two weeks before we took it off. When we did, the toe had grown back, except it was a little bit crooked and remains crooked to this day. The toe didn't slow me down much, though. By Monday, with two socks on that foot and a shoe with the toe cut out, I was back hoeing peanuts for four dollars a day. I couldn't work hay, but by being careful not to hit my toe with my hoe, I could make a hand in the peanuts and cotton fields.

Mr. Hugh Young had given me a tractor inner tube that he had ruined by running over a persimmon sprout. These tubes were hard to come by for a boy. They made the best slingshot rubbers that one could find. It was wartime, and most inner tubes were made of synthetic rubber, but farmers could still get them made of pure latex. Tractor tubes were made thicker than those for cars, and when you cut a narrow strip from one, it was very stout and would stretch as far as one could reach without breaking.

With a pine board I rough cut me a slingshot stock with Daddy's handsaw. Then with my barlow knife I whittled it into a fine stock. I added two of the tractor-tube rubbers and a leather from the tongue of an old shoe, and I was ready for hunting. We made Dick a smaller one and went looking for some other boys to go bull-bat hunting with us. We stopped at the blacksmith shop and filled our pockets with what we called slugs. They were bits and pieces of metal that Mr. Clifton cut from bolts and metal he was working with. The only thing better was ball bearings, but they were hard to come by. Most boys had a few of these that they used in a legging marble game. The heavy steel balls would knock marbles out of the ring and not get stuck themselves.

Jerry, Fonze, and Harry were soon found, and the bull-bat hunt was on. Bull bats are not really bats. They are a large bird that flies late in the evening or just before a rain. They dive from great heights and the feathers of their wings make a deep roar as they cut through the air, sounding like a bullfrog. During the heat of the day, they lay flat on limbs of tall trees about thirty feet above the ground and are very hard to hit with a slingshot. To knock one off the limb is a great shot. But they won't fly, so you can shoot again and again.

Fonze noticed my slingshot rubbers first, and then everyone wanted a pair of them. Dick and I promised they could cut off a pair later. A tractor tube will make enough rubbers for every slingshot in town and still have plenty left over. Our first bull bat was on a limb that ran straight out from a huge cottonwood tree and was about thirty-five feet above the ground. Slugs and rocks began to fly, but it was plain to see that we all were not in very good practice. I selected a nut that Mr. Clifton had cut off of a bolt, took dead aim, and pulled my new rubbers back as far as I could stretch them and let go. I hit just between the limb and the bull bat. Half hurt and half surprised, he fell almost to the ground before he stretched his wings and flew off through the trees.

I was very proud of the first scored hit of the day, even though I didn't have the bull bat to prove it. Actually, I was kinda glad he got away. I really didn't like killing anything that is not used for food. Daddy says that everything has a purpose or reason for living or God would not have put them on the earth. Some animals are for food, and some are to keep everything in balance. I didn't know what is the purpose of a bull bat, other than he ate flying insects that fly just before dark. Perhaps he was like the purple martins that lived in the little houses Daddy made and put on tall poles in our back yard. They were supposed to eat a thousand mosquitoes each day. The bluebirds in the fence post at the corner of our garden picked worms from the cabbages and other vegetables. So I guess bull bats also had their good side. I know when they fly you can shoot a rock close to one and he will dive for the rock, thinking it is a June bug or something. He will fly away when he sees that it is just a rock.

We were not too successful at bull-bat hunting that day. My near hit was the only hit of the day. We did get to shoot at a cottontail rabbit as he scampered off through the woods, but no one hit him. Snowball had left again and had gone back to Turkey John's house, I guess. He would have caught that rabbit had he been with us. I just didn't know what I was going to do about the best dog I had ever owned, in fact the best dog in the whole country. I hate to see a dog tied up all the time. It is against his nature. All dogs used to be wild, like the wolf, until man tamed him. To tie one up would be like putting a bird in a cage or a man in jail. Donnie's dad was in the pen for something, but I didn't know what. He was the strongest man in our town, but behind bars he was as weak as the weakest man, for he was not able to do anything.

Dick and I headed home through Teague's pasture. Wendell was rounding up his milk cows for the evening milking. He was riding old Bell. Bell was a milk cow that Wendell had broke to ride. He would put a saddle on her like a horse and use only a rope around her neck and half-hitched around her nose to guide her by. He rode her to round up the other cows. We didn't yell at Wendell, for he would come over and talk an hour, and we needed to get home and do our own chores.

As we walked under a bois d'arc tree, I spotted a dove on her nest. I hadn't been too pleased with my shooting that day, so I just took a practice shot at her with a slug in my slingshot. To my great surprise and anguish, I had hit her right on the head. She fell out of the nest and straight to the ground without even a flutter. Daddy had told us boys never to kill a dove because they were sacred birds. It was a dove that came back to the ark to tell Noah that the water was going down after the great flood. The dove brought back proof of land to show Noah. Now I had killed one dead just for a practice shot.

I grabbed up the dove and ran over to a waterhole and bathed her head with water, but it was of no use. She was dead as a doornail. I felt guilty and made Dick promise that he would never tell a soul about it. If Daddy found out, he would strap me good with the double razor strap that hung on his dresser mirror. I never knew if it was the sting of the strap or the pop of the double leather that made it so effective, but it sure was. We boys had rather take Mom's peach-tree limb any day. I also felt bad about the two eggs in the nest that she was setting on. Now they could never hatch and grow up to be sacred birds. Today men go dove hunting all the time, even eat their breast meat. But I have never been able to shoot another one, and I never shall. Dick and I dug a hole beside the trail and buried the dove. I felt that was the least I could do.

After chores and supper, with about an hour's daylight left, Dick and I took some pork meat rind and some string over to the ditch that ran at the back of the schoolyard and by Bill Williams' place. With a piece of meat rind tied onto a string and a fence staple or nail through it for weight, we began to catch some of the biggest red crawfish (we called them wire pinchers) I had ever seen. We soon caught a bucket almost full. They would clamp their large pinchers onto the meat rind and would not turn loose in time, and we would lift them up out of the water and over our bucket. They usually dropped off into the bucket without us having to touch them with our hands.

When we had enough, we began to clean their tails. They are much better to eat than salt-water shrimp. Before we went to bed that night, we salted them, rolled them in cornmeal, and fried them. The whole family had a good bedtime snack of fresh crawfish before we went to bed. I read about a chapter in my book, *The U.P. Trail* by Zane Grey, before I turned out my flashlight to go to sleep. I still felt bad about killing the sacred bird.

Chapter XII

FISHING WITH TURKEY JOHN

Dick caught a fever. Daddy said, "From too much swimming in cow ponds." Joe had gone to the big city for the rest of the summer to work for the Armour Star Company. This was the week we were supposed to go to Turkey John's. July had come, and all the crops were laid-by awaiting harvest. Our garden was all about over except for the okra and melons. Our truck patch of potatoes had been dug, and the potatoes were in the barn. The jumbo peanuts and popcorn were not yet ready, and the field corn looked good and would be ready about September 1. So Daddy said that I could go spend a week with Turkey John. He knew how much I had planned for the stay and also how much I missed my dog. Snowball was now a permanent member of Turkey John's family.

So on that Monday, the first full week in July, I rode my bike to Red River. Mom had packed my luggage rack with canned peaches and stuff for Turkey John, and I had taken one change of clothes by her urging. I doubted that I would need them, as

I would wear only my pants and I would be in and out of the river fishing and swimming so much I would just wash them right on me and let them dry the same way.

I arrived at Turkey John's a little before noon. He had already run his lines and nets for the morning and was sitting in the shade watching the river roll by. Bobang (Snowball) lay beside him, but got up and greeted me as if I were a long-lost friend. He said that the water "helped him think." He was glad to see me but had "figured out I would come today." He didn't say how he had figured it out, and I didn't ask. He was glad for the peaches and stuff. He said, "Big cat running our bank and need you help get carp bait to catch him. After eat we go seine."

Lunch was cold fried squirrel, bread, and coffee, but it was good, and peddling that three or four miles had made me hungry. After we finished eating, we took the seine and walked downriver about a quarter of a mile to an old slew mouth. The water was about waist deep on me. We unrolled the seine. It had a pole on each end to hold onto and keep the lead line on the bottom and was about twenty feet long. We made one swing out into the slew and then back to the bank. We caught six carp about the size of one's hand and about half of a bucket of shiner minnows and some small shad. Turkey John said, "That plenty bait for week."

On the way back to "camp" (as Turkey John

called it), he taught me how to tell a wolf track from a dog track. He showed me a fox track and also a bobcat. He took us by a tree hanging full of ripe possum grapes. We both helped ourselves to the large bunches of grapes hanging there. They were sure sweet and good. Turkey John chewed his up, seed, skin, and all, and swallowed them. I chewed them just enough to get the juice out of them and spit them out. He said, "Swallow them. They good for belly." Perhaps so, but I still spit them out. He laughed, and grabbed the buckets and started off up the river. I quickly followed with the seine.

We stopped dead still in the path that the cows had made along the river bank. Turkey John pointed out two cat squirrels at play in the top of a cottonwood tree. They hadn't heard us coming or they would have been gone, because cat squirrels are about the quickest things in the wild. If a dog should tree one, they just leap from tree to tree until they get back to their den tree, then run into their hole. They move so fast you don't have time to take aim at them with a gun. To hunt them you have to "still hunt," where you just sit down hidden and wait for them to come out of the hole. They sure are good fried or stewed with dumplings in with them.

When we got back to camp, we loaded our two bait buckets in the long flat-bottom boat, along with hooks, lines, and some weights for the lines to hold them down close to the bottom. Turkey John sat in the middle seat for the oaring, and I was in the back seat. I started to get into the front seat, but he said, "It easier to row when bow out of water." Turkey John sat facing me because that's the way oars operate.

We headed at an angle across the river, pointing the boat some upstream. I quickly saw that we were moving straight across the river. He had to row against the current of the water or it would take us downriver. When we reached the other side, he oared us up under some willow trees. He tied a drop hook to one of the overhanging limbs and put a minnow on the hook. We repeated this until all the drop hooks were set. Sometimes Turkey John would bait with a shad and sometimes with a minnow. He said, "Big flat-head cat on these come morning."

We headed back across the river. We had worked our way upriver, so when we got to the Oklahoma bank we were quite a ways above camp. The Oklahoma bank, was a high red-clay bluff, and the water ran deep and much slower along that bank. We came to a large cottonwood tree that had fallen into the river but whose roots were still holding onto the clay. Turkey John grabbed one of the limbs and handed it back to me and said, "Hold on." Then without any warning he slipped over the side and disappeared down into the water. He made no splash or noise.

It seemed like he was gone an awful long time. I just knew he had drowned down there or some old alligator gar had bitten off his arm or legs or something. But finally he came up about twenty feet from the boat. He said, "This good set for line. Big cat been here."

"Now how can you tell?" I asked.

He said, "Fish like other wild things. They feed same trail. Old cat rub nose on bottom scaring up bait. He leave trail. Water deep and slow here, sand not race out trail. We catch him on third hook from log."

"Will we catch him tonight?" I asked.

"Don't know. Big fish don't run every night. If him caught big bait, him lay in hole or under log maybe two, three days."

We tied our line to one of the big limbs of the cottonwood down below water. We pinned the carp on the hooks through their back so they would stay alive on the hook. We put on two window weights along the line to keep it on bottom and a large weight on the end to keep the line stretched out tight. After setting the line we then headed back to camp. I was amazed that Turkey John sat with his back to the front of the boat but never looked round. Yet he pulled us right into our boat dock at camp. He sure knew that river. Also, when he brought the oars forward and put them down into the water, there was never a splash or sound. When he pulled on the oars, the boat pushed forward with great force.

Bobang was on the bank when we pulled into the dock. He had been off hunting when we left and didn't go with us. He was very glad to see us. He jumped into the river and swam out to meet the boat. Turkey John helped him into the boat, and he went straight to the bow, even though he only got to ride a few feet back to the dock.

We caught some grasshoppers out in a meadow just north of camp to do some bank fishing with a pole that night. Turkey John said there would be a good moon and we would catch some channel catfish. So after a supper of fried bacon, gravy, and hoecake bread, we sat on the bank with a long pole and a line and hook on it baited with grasshoppers. Sure enough, each grasshopper we had caught began to produce a nice channel catfish. We caught them and dropped them into the live box for safekeeping.

At bedtime I had to be assured that no rattlesnake had slid down the flue during the day before I spread my blanket on the floor of the dugout. I soon was snug in my blanket with Bobang laying beside me. Turkey John was in a talking mood and began to tell me about the river before all the farmers moved in to farm the bottom land. Lots of deer and turkey were here then. He was still talking when I went to sleep.

When I awoke, the dugout door was wide open, and daylight was pouring in. I could smell coffee and hear bacon sizzling in a skillet. When I appeared up the steps of the dugout, Turkey John said, "Boy it gonna be hot, but maybe we get breeze from south across river and keep us cool."

After breakfast, Turkey John said, "We go

see if we got big fish." So we loaded the boat. This time Bobang jumped in and went to the bow end. One time he bailed off into the water to chase a beaver, but the old beaver went under and came up about one hundred feet downriver. Turkey John helped Bobang back into the boat. Then Bobang went back to the bow and shook his coat until we both got wet. Turkey John laughed and said, "You catch Mr. Beaver, Bobang? You don't like beaver, do you, Bobang?" The dog wouldn't even look around, as if he knew that Turkey John was making fun of him.

We went straight up the Oklahoma bank toward the big cottonwood tree. Even before we got there, I could see the limbs on the tree jerking. I yelled, "We got him, Uncle," and for the first time he turned around and looked.

He said, "We have to be quiet and not spook him. He pull hook out of mouth or break line."

We eased up, and I slipped a line around a limb of the tree to hold the boat. Turkey John took a cotton rope with a huge hook on it and tied it to a metal eye bolt on the side of the boat, then he slipped gently over the side and was gone.

It seemed like he was gone forever. Finally he came up and said, "We got two big cat. One about fifty pound and one about thirty-five pound. I put gaff hook in big one mouth, but we lose other when we pull him up. If I could get small hook out of his mouth, we could save both, but he swallowed it with bait." He swam there with only his head out of the water for a long time, then reached into a sack he had on his boat seat and got a big hunting knife and put it in his mouth and went down again.

When he cut the line that fastened the hook to the main line, the big fish began to pull on the rope and pulled the boat upstream. I had it tied good to the tree limb, so all he could do was pull the front of the boat back and forth. Turkey John slipped over the side of the boat back onto his seat and began to pull in the rope. Soon the big fish was alongside of the boat. With one hand holding the rope, he put his other arm down around the fish and held him against the boat. Then, when the fish was quiet, he rolled him over into the boat. I am sure that was not the first time he ever did that, because he did it with such ease. He then tied another rope through the big cat's mouth and gills and tied him to the boat seat and unhooked the big gaff hook. With the rope and gaff hook in his hand, he slipped over the side again, and soon I was feeling the other fish pulling on the boat.

Turkey John followed the same procedure to load the second catfish and tied him to the boat seat the same way as the other one. We rebaited the line with live carp and reset it back where it was. But instead of heading across the river to check the drop lines, we went back down the river to the boat dock and put the two big cats in the live box for safe-keeping. We reloaded into the boat and oared across the river to the willow trees. There we found two fish. One was a flat-head cat and one a channel cat. While we were over there, we rebaited everything and checked one hoop net that Turkey John had tied to a log in the middle of the river. I recognized the net as one of the nets that my daddy had knitted for him back in the wintertime. There were two big buffalo fish in the net. Turkey John baited his nets with cottonseed cake (that was cotton seed after the oil has been cooked and pressed out of it). This was hung inside the net in a sack from the top of the net. Turkey John took the fish out of the net and dropped it back down into the river and we headed back to camp. When Turkey John put the two catfish and the two buffalo in the live box, he said, "Best fishing in many moon. You bring me good luck."

"All I did was help you seine the bait," I said.

"Tomorrow big politician coming from city to buy fish. Him say he take all I got. Him want to have a big fish fry to help get votes. We have him big mess of fish, huh?"

I was really hoping we would go see the new wild horse Turkey John had caught, but I knew he would have to stay here and wait on the politician. I dropped the gallus of my overalls and ran for the boat dock, diving like a bullfrog into the river. I swam out about fifty yards to where the water was only about waist deep. Turkey John laughed and followed me, clothes and all. He was a good swimmer. I had learned to swim a couple years before, the hard way. My brother Joe had thrown me in

Tuckalo Creek and told me to swim or drown. I managed to dog paddle my way back to the bank, swallowing about a gallon of water. I was mad enough at my brother that I would have killed him if I could have only caught him, but I couldn't. He was six years older than I was and could outrun me. But after that I wasn't ever afraid of water again and became a pretty good swimmer.

The next morning I took Turkey John's rifle and Snowball and I went squirrel hunting. Turkey John was going to run the lines, then he would wait for the politician to come get the fish. This worried me, because most people that came and bought fish from Turkey John would bring a bottle and give him several drinks before they bought the fish. They knew he would sell the fish much cheaper if he was drunk. Also, once he started drinking, he couldn't quit. He would take all the money he had and go buy liquor until all his money was gone or until he was so weak he couldn't get up and go get another drink. I knew that someday all this would kill him.

When I returned with two squirrels for dinner, Turkey John was sitting looking into the water. When he heard me coming, he arose with a grin. Then he reached into his pocket and pulled out a handful of money. He had over a hundred dollars he had gotten from selling the fish. The man had given Turkey John a bottle, but he hadn't drank a drop of it. He didn't drink all that week–I guess because I was there. He said that he also might have a buyer for the big black horse. He was to come back in a few weeks and try him out.

Wednesday morning we got up early, and after we had our breakfast, we walked the mile or so down the river to the horse trap where the new pinto horse was kept. Before we got there, I could see her standing in the corral. She sure was a pretty horse. She was red and white spotted. The red was brighter than most paint horses. Turkey John said, "You stay back until I tell Buckchee that you are here. She might get excited." So I stopped where I was but could see the horse real well. Turkey John walked up to the corral, talking to the horse all the time, in Cherokee, I think. He stepped into the corral and slipped a fishing cord around the horse's neck and slipped up onto her back. He rode her around the corral several times, guiding her only by the cord on her neck. By this time I was up sitting on the corral fence watching in unbelief that he could be riding a wild horse with nothing but a fishing cord around her neck.

He rode over to where I was and slid off her back and handed me the cord. "You ride," he said. I was a little frightened at first, but once I slipped off the corral fence onto her back and saw how gentle she was, I truly enjoyed the ride. Usually I am not much of a horse-riding person myself. I prefer my bike.

Turkey John said, "She ready, and now me sell big black stallion. Me want colt from him first.

Might get me black and white paint. Both strong horses and Black, him big and tall. Colt should be good horse."

We didn't go back to camp along the river bank as we had come, but cut north into the river-bottom timber. There were big, tall cottonwood, ash, blackjack, oak, and hackberry. These woods had never been logged. It was just like it was before the white man came and cleared land for farming and logged the big timber for lumber. We went by two rabbit gums (traps) and a quail trap. They all had game in them. We had meat enough for the rest of the week. We then went into the edge of Mr. A. Goodman's cornfield and gathered some fresh roasting ears. We both ate one raw, as it was getting close to lunch time and we were hungry. I asked Turkey John, "Isn't this stealing?" He said that he did lots of work for Mr. A. and he had told him to get corn for himself and for his horse whenever he wanted it.

Next to the cornfield was a watermelon patch, and we found one that was ripe. You can tell by the little curly vine just next to the melon. When that turns brown, the melon is ripe. We cut the melon with my barlow knife and feasted on the sweet juicy red meat of the melon. Again Turkey John ate seed and all. We ate our fill and headed on home with the corn, rabbits, and quail.

The week passed much too fast, and Saturday came and I had to go home. I missed my home some, but I sure could have stayed another week or so with Turkey John. I had learned so much about how to live in the wild and how to recognize wild things by tracks and movement in the woods. I had also learned a lot about fishing. I am not sure I could ever become a dugout dwelling fisherman, but I sure did like the big river. Turkey John sent Daddy a nice catfish he had saved for him. He sent Dick an Indian bow he had made of bois d'arc wood and strung with strong fishing cord. He sent Mom some money to buy material for a new dress.

I was glad to be home again. I left Snowball with Turkey John. I knew that if I towed him home on a cord again, he would just go right back. He was the best dog I had ever owned, and I never forgot him.

Joe came home from the city in time for summer school, but he never stayed home much after that. He soon finished school and joined the army, leaving for good. Dick got over his fever and fell from the truck that hauled us to the field to work. The back wheel ran over Dick's leg and bruised his leg bone. The doctor had to go in and scrape the bone. Dick limped all through the school year.

Word came to my classroom that my dad was sick. He had a stroke from which he never recovered, leaving Mom, Charlene, Dick, and I to fend for ourselves.

We didn't mind the work in the fields so bad but could not always find work to do so, provisions at our house would get kinda low. Yet we made it somehow. We always had chickens when we got meat hungry and canned fruit and vegetables and onions and potatoes we had raised. We also continued to raise jumbo peanuts and popcorn for winter snack food.

No matter how low provisions got at our house, we were a happy family. Happiness is not related to what you own but in relationship to one another.

Chapter XIII

WORK TRIP TO SOUTHWEST OKLAHOMA

Summer was soon over, and memories of my two-week stay with Turkey John lingered on. It would be easy for a boy to set a goal of spending his life fishing on a river bank somewhere and living always close to nature. And it would be easy to forget some of the hardships of that kind of life, like last spring when it rained so much that the river came out of its banks and filled John's dugout with mud and sand. It took days after it went back into banks to clean up the mud. He finally found his boat over two miles downriver caught in a pile of driftwood in the middle of the river. I guess that everything good has a price that has to be paid.

Summer school had some changes. I was in a different room with a different teacher. It was a man teacher (my first), and the story spread throughout the school that he used a paddle in his left hand and could really make a believer of you right quick. I decided that I didn't want to try him to find out. I would just stay out of trouble.

He seemed to be nice enough. We always began class with the Pledge of Allegiance to the flag. Then we all repeated the Lord's Prayer together. We could do that back then, and no one seemed to care. It was the Supreme Court that stopped it. Then we would sing two or three songs together. I always liked that time. Since I ordered the book from which to learn to play the guitar, singing was something I enjoyed doing.

The fifth and sixth grade was in the same room. The teacher couldn't give each one of us much of his time, but while the sixth grade was having a subject I listened and learned from then. So when I got up to that grade it wasn't very hard. I had finally caught up with my grade level in arithmetic. I had struggled since my teacher, the school superintendent, and the county superintendent decided to promote me from the second grade to the fourth grade. I had missed the multiplication tables and how to do long division. These were hard to catch up. There were four of us that this had happened to, and we pulled together or we would not have made it.

Soon summer school was out, and we were back in the farmers' fields hunting something to do to make some money. My brogan shoes were worn out. There was a hole in the sole of the left one, and both of them were cracked up pretty badly. Also, I needed winter clothes, though my coat would make another season. I always bought my coat a little too large so I could wear it for two winters. Last year I bought a heavy Mackinaw, and it was in pretty good shape.

Then, summer was gone, and fall harvest time came. Dick and I could make good money in the cotton fields. There were other things to harvest, but none as plentiful as cotton. Peanut harvest paid more per day, but only lasted about three weeks, where cotton would last all fall, even up past the cold frost that came in November. I have even picked cotton at Christmas time.

Cotton grew in rows, and the field would turn a solid white when the burrs were open and it was ready to pick. Scales for weighing up sacks of cotton would be set up on a tripod in the middle of the field. When your sack was full, you would put it across your shoulder and carry it to the scales to determine the weight. Farmers who trusted their workers (hands) would let them weigh their own sacks and record the weight in the scale book. This book was used to determine how much each worker was due in wages and to determine how much to put on the wagon or truck to haul to the cotton gin. When the trash and seeds were ginned out, the farmer was working toward a five-hundred-pound of lint to make up a bale.

If the workers were not trusted by the farmer, his wife or someone was kept at the scales to read the weights and record the weights in the book used to keep each person's work and keep the bale total.

Also at the scales there was a water keg. It would be wrapped in burlap and kept damp, so the evaporation would keep the water cool. A dipper gourd full of that cool water sure tasted good and renewed one's strength. Each worker would also keep his own weights. This would be for the purpose of keeping day-by-day totals of weights and wages. These little books were supplied by the cotton gin or at a retail store supplied by a tobacco company for advertising purposes.

To prepare for the season Dick and I painted the bottom of our sacks black to make them wear longer and pull easier. And we put a round steel ring on a tail strap used to tie up the bottom, so one could empty the sack from both ends, and the ring was used to hang the sack on the scales.

Dick and I would take three rows together. This created a competition trying to get as much of the center row as we could, because the one who got the most of the center row would be the one who would weigh up the heavier sack at the scales.

We had been picking about three weeks when a man from southwestern Oklahoma came to offer us a job. If Dick and I would go home with him, he would pay us five dollars each, per day, to help him milk twenty-seven cows in a grade-A raw-milk dairy, and also give us plenty of time each day to pull cotton. Mr. Wadsworth said that he would put up two army cots in his storm cellar and we could sleep there.

We would have about four weeks to work if we stayed a few days past the school beginning in November.

We packed our work clothes into an old cardboard suitcase. At this time of the year all our clothes could be classified as work clothes. They had a full winter's wear on them with knee patches and all.

We loaded into Mr. Wadsworth's car, taking care to take our straw hats and new cotton sacks. The trip took about three and one-half hours, ending at a farm along the north bank of the north fork of Red River. Though the land all along the river bank was sand dunes and not farmable, the further you got from the water's edge, the more fertile the land got until the cotton fields were solid white and alfalfa to bale for the dairy cows was rank and green. He used the river sand grass to graze the cows on during the day, while the hay meadows grew.

We unloaded what we brought in the big concrete cellar. There was plenty room for two cots and a card table for an eating table. We had stopped a few miles down the road from the farm and bought a supply of canned foods. Mom had also sent some jars of peaches, green beans, etc. The farmer's house was next door, and the boss had said that we would take part of our meals at the big house. So far we had found the boss to be a good, honest man. We also had all the good fresh milk that we could drink. Dick and I figured that if we worked two extra weeks after school started we would be able to take about two hundred and fifty dollars each home to help with the needs of the home and have some spending money to buy our winter shoes and clothing.

We had never been this far from home before by ourselves, so it was an adventure for us and also a time to prove to ourselves and to others that we could make it on our own.

The first evening we observed Mr. Wadsworth milking and helped him put the cows in the lot and clean up the barn. We used a high-pressure water hose to wash down the barn. The floor was concrete and was not hard to clean. We then bottled the milk and put it in the walk-in refrigerator for the next morning's delivery.

When morning came we were on our own. We opened the gate between the lot and barn, and the cows got in line to be milked. They would line up the same way every milking. I don't know if the farmer trained them to line up that way or if they trained themselves, but they did it the same way every time on their own.

When the milking was complete, cooled out, then bottled, and the barn was cleaned, we grabbed our cotton sacks and headed for the field. We took a small lunch so we could work until milking time again (about 4 p.m.). By this time in the morning the dew had dried off the cotton stalks, and one could straddle the row and strip the cotton from the bottom of the stalk to the top with both hands, then put it all in the mouth of the sack. This was the greater difference between picking cotton and pulling bowls. Picking had to be mostly done with one hand removing the white cotton from each burr and holding the stalk with the other hand, while pulling could be done with both hands at once removing cotton, burrs, and even some of the dead leaves.

We would pull until 4 p.m., and in that length of time we could weigh in about five hundred pounds. Dick always beat me by twenty-five to fifty pounds. He was smaller and much more agile than I, though I was two years older and outweighed him several pounds. But my weight worked against me in this type of work. Now in hauling hay and work like that I was the better hand because I could lift and handle the heavier weights.

We were paid five dollars each for our milking chore, then we made about ten dollars each day in the cotton patch, but it made a long, hard day. Yet we were making more money than any kid our age. When we were finally finished with the evening milking, it would be a long, hard day. Our parents had taught us to work, so long, hard hours didn't hurt us so much. We ate a can of pork and beans and a Spam or potted-meat sandwich and drank a quart of cold milk from the milk barn and got into bed. We had a small radio to listen to and I had brought a couple books to read, but it didn't take long before we were sound asleep. It didn't seem long before that old wind-up alarm clock was telling us it was milking time. Boy, how we missed Mom's hot breakfasts but, with a quick sandwich and a piece of fruit and a glass of milk, we were on our way to the barn. About halfway through the milking the boss would come and load out his delivery van with cold milk for his morning route. It wasn't long until our chores were done, and we were headed for the cotton patch.

The third day we were there, a family came in an old cloth-top car with an Arkansas tag on it, looking for work. They were headed for California to find a permanent job but had car trouble and spent their traveling money on the car, so they needed to work a while to make enough money to get them to California. There was a man and wife and six kids, and the wife was expecting their seventh child very soon.

I asked them to wait until the boss got back from his milk route. He might have some work pulling cotton for them to make enough to get them to California. The boss also had a sharecroppers house that no one lived in, and it would keep them dry and warm if a cold spell came. It had a wood heater that would keep the cabin warm, and they could cook on the top of it. It wasn't long before the boss returned and loaned them a couple of cotton sacks and told them to feel free to get vegetables from the garden and to live in the little sharecropper's house. They didn't have a thing. Where I came from, there were lots of poor people, but I had never before seen people as poor as this family from Arkansas.

They had a boy named Victor. He was about our age. We called him Vic. He took up with Dick and me and would come by the cellar each evening when our work was done to listen to our radio or listen to me read a chapter in my book. Vic could not read or write, so hearing a book read was quite a treat for him. I couldn't imagine how folks could make it without knowing how to read. I was very interested in *Moby Dick*. Through the pages of the book I could escape the present and adventure out on the rough sea in search of a white killer whale. Or in the *Call of the Wild* I could travel in my mind to Alaska where it was fifty degrees below zero and the creek beds in the spring had flakes of gold in them. All one had to do was pan it out of the mud and water. Life would be awfully dull if it wasn't for the books I read. During the summer months I had read *The Adventures of Tom Sawyer* and enjoyed my trip deep into the river cave and my raft trip on the big river.

We worked every day that week except

Sunday. We were taught that Sunday was a holy day and one should rest on that day. Yet the milking was necessary labor (ox in the ditch, Dad would call it), so we did the regular milking and cleaning of the barn but took the rest of the day off. Dick and Vic went to the river to swim. I saddled the boss's paint horse and took his .22 rifle to go see if I could kill a goose or duck. Dick and Vic went up river to swim, so I rode down the river to get out of rifle range with them. Soon I spotted some geese down the river setting on a sand bar. Something scared them before I could slip up on them even though I was horseback, and geese aren't afraid of horses. I had a row of willows between me and the geese. Out walked the Arkansawyer. I got one shot and got a goose, but the rest of them flew on down the river.

I rode out to the sand bar and got the goose, then rode on down the river. I hadn't been riding long until I came upon a two-thirds grown rabbit. When I got back to the Arkansawyer's house, I gave him the rabbit to make a pot of stew out of. Then I took the goose to Mrs. Wadsworth. Monday night she invited Dick and me over for goose and dressing. It sure was good.

We had worked four and a half weeks each and had made about three hundred apiece, but we needed to get home and get in school. Mr. Wadsworth took us to Altus to catch the Greyhound bus. The trip home didn't seem so long because of our desire to be there. We stopped in several towns, including Ardmore, where we had lunch. I ate a bowl of stew, as I had eaten all the sandwiches that I wanted while I slept in the cellar.

We got off the bus in Bokchito, still about twelve miles from home. No main highway went through our little town. It wasn't long before we caught a ride on a logging truck that was hauling logs out of Red River bottom. They went right by where we lived. We both were sure glad to get home. We greeted our daddy, mother, and little sister. Joe wasn't home yet from his summer job in Oklahoma City. We gave Mother most of the money that we had made. Daddy was old and ill and unable to furnish the keep for our home, except a small old-age assistance check he got from the state each month.

We kids had learned well how to work, so we hired ourselves out to the farmers for wages. Mom also went with us if it was something that she was able to do, like hoeing rows of cotton, corn, or peanuts. In the fall she could pick some cotton, but she had a painful kidney and couldn't do much of it. But with the wages Dick and I brought home, we would have money for school clothes and supplies. We would have some left for Christmas and emergency needs. Dick and I were proud that we were able to help our family with some of our financial needs. It meant we were growing up some.

Chapter XIV

FIFTH GRADE BEGINS

School was about the same as when we left. There was some change in enrollment, as in the rural farm county there would be some movement of sharecroppers. Land owners were always looking for better farmers to tend their land, and sharecroppers were always looking for more fertile ground and a better house to live in, better schools for their kids, and better farm equipment to work with. Some land owners would furnish teams of horses or a tractor to work with.

Often times the sharecroppers' kids wouldn't be new to the community. They may have been gone a couple of years, then returned to the same farm or another one in the community. One family who had lived there before moved in across the road from us. The house had a huge barn behind it and it was a great place for kids to play and also to learn great lessons. One lesson was you cannot jump out of the barn loft with an umbrella and expect to float down. The umbrella will turn wrong side out and the fall to the cow lot is a hard one.

The kids were Marlene and Freddie. Marlene was my age, and Freddie was Dick's age. We played well together. The barn had a long, sloping roof of sheet iron, and with a piece of cardboard to sit on, one could make a very fast trip from the top to the bottom. The drop to the ground wasn't a long one, and you could land on your feet. A ladder provided a means to get back up on the barn roof, and our new rubber-sole brogan shoes helped us to run up to the top of the barn for another trip down. There were a great number of games and things that farm kids can find to do.

One Saturday we all got together at my house, and with Dad providing the engineering and Joe as the main work director, we built what was called a flying jennie. It was a big post put into the ground about three feet deep, then cut off until about three feet stood out of the ground. We then used a 2x10 board about twenty feet long. A hole was drilled in the center of the board. A large bridge nail was used to fasten the board to the top of the post with a large washer between them. It was greased with wagon grease. Then a boy would sit on each end, and someone would spin the board as fast as they could and see which boy could hold his seat the longest.

Another fun thing was a cable tied near the top of a large oak tree that was easy to climb. It ran down the hill about two hundred yards to another tree just high enough one came down on his feet. A well pulley was used to hook over the cable, and with a boy holding onto a cross bar, he would climb the big oak, hook the pulley over the cable, and ride it down to the bottom. The next boy would then take the pulley and repeat the trip. Hours could be spent before one knew it, playing with one of these things we had built.

School hadn't changed much since the summer session. Our classroom had been moved to the large room on the north side of the gym stage. Our teacher was Mr. Teague, the first man teacher I ever had. He was a good man but demanded much from each of us. Dad had us to bring our books home each evening so we could catch up on the studies that we missed while we were in western Oklahoma and to make good grades under this new teacher. Dad had a vision of us kids going to college and knew that good grades could be our means of a scholarship.

Dad also changed his mind about my extra reading and allowed me to keep the light on to read as long as I cared to at night. He did ask to see the book I was reading from time to time to make sure I was reading wholesome literature.

Aunt Hattie was coming to see us for Thanksgiving. She was Daddy's sister and lived in Telephone, Texas. Telephone wasn't far, as a crow flies, but the great cable bridge that used to cross the river between our county and Telephone was destroyed during the bridge war. Oklahoma by the

"Louisiana Purchase" owned Red River to the southern water's edge, but Texas charged a toll to cross all the bridges. Three of the cable bridges fell in one night by somebody pouring acid on the cables. One main bridge had its road plowed up on the Oklahoma side, and the Oklahoma National Guard was ordered by the governor to guard the north end, while the Texas Rangers guarded the south end.

The federal government stepped in for the sake of peace and negotiated an agreement between the two states. But in the agreement the Telephone bridge and the Sowell Bluff bridge were never rebuilt. To this day you cannot go directly across the river to Telephone, and it lengthened the trip by fifty-plus miles.

Also, Turkey John came for Thanksgiving and brought a fifteen-pound catfish. We heated a pot of water to scald the fish. Daddy didn't like a skinned fish. He said that all the flavor was in the skin, so we scalded and scraped the catfish then cut him up to fry.

Company at our house was always a time for a big celebration. The-old timers say "it was time to put the big pot into the little pot," meaning it was a time for a big feast. Dad had fattened an old hen for hen and dressing. Mom would cook pumpkin pies and peach cobbler. She would also open jars of canned vegetables. Aunt Hattie was always a delight-ful person and brought us up on the happenings of her side of the family. She always brought us kids a package of Juicyfruit gum, which made a great hit with us. She would stay two or three days until one of her family came and got her. We had no car. Years back we had a Ford, but when times were hard, Daddy had to sell the car to help with the household needs.

Turkey John said that he had caught some nice fish that summer and fall but none as large as the two that he and I caught. He was now riding the paint mare and had sold the big black horse. He was hoping for a colt from her in the early summer and wished for a black and white colt.

Thanksgiving was a great day. The big walnut table was covered with food, and everyone had a great time. Turkey John told me that Bobang got rattlesnake bit. He was a very sick dog for days, but John kept a plaster of crushed herbs on the bite to draw the poison out. The dog got well. I don't know what the roots and herbs were that John used, but Indians just knew things like that.

The season had changed until each morning everything was covered with white frost. Much of the time we would have ice on the chicken's watering trough and have to draw a fresh bucket of water for the chickens before we went to school. Our well was sixty feet deep, so to draw a bucket of water was no easy task. But one got use to it, and then it wasn't so hard.

It also was time to heat the house with the

old wood heater, so Joe, Dick, and I spent a lot of Saturdays going to the woods and cutting ash, oak, and hackberry logs to haul into the wood lot. There we would put a log in the saw rack and cut it into twenty-four-inch lengths to split into heater wood. Somehow Daddy would know when a bad cold spell was coming, and he would have us cut a lot of extra wood and stack it on the east porch to keep it dry and have it where it was easy to carry into the house and put in the wood box.

On cold winter evenings we would pop corn, or parch peanuts and sit up and play games. Some evenings Dick and I would go to Jerry's house and listen to Jack, Doc, and Reggie solve a mystery on the radio program "I Love a Mystery," or some other radio program. Daddy went to bed early and wouldn't allow us to listen to the radio after he went to bed.

On Thursday, after the first of December, there was a hard freeze. Friday was even colder, so we school kids decided to go to Williams' pond Saturday to skate. We didn't have ice skates, so we would run full speed down the dam, then skate on our shoes all the way across the pond. Several fell and hit their head pretty hard, but it didn't stop our skating. After we had been there a while, several girls showed up to skate with us. In the past we would have resented girls joining our fun times, but things were changing and we didn't seem to mind the girls being with us. In fact, we kinda enjoyed teaching them how to skate and would help them up when they fell.

After a couple hours skating we went over to one of the girl's house where her mother made us all some hot chocolate. Dick and I excused ourselves after a bit because we had wood to cut and school homework to do at home.

Chapter XV

THE BLACK PANTHER

One night down in the river bottom where there is a number of sharecropper farms, a great scream was heard by several families. They all reported it about the same. It moved slowly down through the river bottom, stopping and screaming at periodic intervals. None of the farmers ever had any dealings with a panther, but all agreed that was what they heard.

The community discussion among the men was whether the panther was just moving through the country or if he was there to stay. Panthers were bad to kill calves and sheep. That seems to be their main food supply, and they've been known to attack humans.

Everyone decided to wait a week and if they continued to hear him, or if there were some live-stock kills, they would form a hunting party with hunters and dogs and go after him. That was one hunt I had no desire to go on. I remember last year when we were possum hunting and the dogs treed something that we had never seen before. It jumped out of the tree and ran. All the dogs gave chase for a little ways but soon returned. It was a big bobcat. A panther is as large as three or four bobcats, and I sure didn't want to face one of them.

Two evenings later, Bottlee was riding in from the bottom and something frightened his horse. The old big black horse reared and bolted down the road. It took a while to pull him to a stop. Bottlee tied up his horse and took his rifle and walked back down the road where his horse first bolted. There was a large pecan tree with a limb that hung out across the road. He saw where the big cat had climbed down the back of the tree and jumped off, leaving a good set of footprints in the damp dirt and leaves before loping off through the woods.

Well, they have an answer now as to what made the screaming noise, even though no one had really seen him. In the west they were called puma or mountain lions and were a reddish yellow to a gray in color, but in the deep south they were black in color and called panthers. No one really knew what color this one was, but they knew it was a large one by the tracks he left.

News went out through the community about Bottlee's encounter with the cat, so it was decided they would all meet at the big pecan tree on Friday night on their horses and would bring all their hunting dogs. No one really had a cat hunting dog, only coon dogs and wolf hounds and a few fox hounds. One farmer had a bloodhound that he was going to bring.

When they were all gathered, there were fifteen men on horses and twenty-seven hound dogs. Then there was a flat-bed truck with myself and several men who had come to hear the chase. Daddy wouldn't let Dick come, but said I could go if I would stay with the truck.

It took about an hour for the hounds to find the cat's trail. Then the chase was on. Mr. Lewis Land, who owned the truck, drove us down the bottom road until we were next to the ash flats. There we could hear the chase good. But at times they would run completely out of sound distance. Once or twice they took him across the river into Texas and back. It was real exciting to hear the hounds and the hunters' horns that were sounded to encourage the dogs.

The chase lasted over three hours, but finally they treed him about two miles east of where we had the truck parked. Mr. Lewis yelled, "Load up. They have treed, and we will get as close as we can." We drove within two hundred yards of where they were. It was at the mouth of Blue River, where it ran into Red River. He was right in the top of a big cottonwood tree. They waited a little while until all the horsemen gathered in. The hounds were bawling and trying to climb the tree as high as they could. Then Bottlee took the 30-30 rifle out of the scabbard and picked him a good location where he could see the cat good and asked for all the lights (most men had carbide lights, some had long five- or eight-cell battery lights).

One man shined his light on the rifle sights so Bottlee could see them, and all the rest of the lights were on the cat. He was coal black and about ten feet long. He was growling and spitting at the dogs and wasn't paying much attention to all the men. One crack from the 30-30 was all it took. The big cat came rolling out of the tree and hit the ground. Every dog jumped on him, but they were not needed because he was dead when he hit the ground.

Men began to grab dogs and snap chains on their collars. Soon all the dogs were caught, and we could move up and get a close look at the panther. He was a male about five years old, some said. His fur was slick black, not a blemish on him.

They loaded him on the truck to haul back to town for everyone to see. It was agreed that Bottlee would get the hide to tan for a rug, after everyone had seen it. The next day almost everyone in town came to Mr. Lewis's store to see the cat. None of us had ever seen a black panther and wanted to know what it looked like. He was bigger than most thought he would be.

The cat was the center of most conversations for a long time to come. And even today, years later, the old-timers sit around, whittling and telling the story of the big cat hunt. The story seems to grow a little each year. Bottlee moved to California and took the black-panther-skin rug with him, so we never got to see it again and there was no way to prove or deny the old gents' stories, of how big he was. But really no one would dare refute the old gents' stories for that would be disrespectful. One thing about country people is that they honor their elders. They call them Mr. and Mrs., or if they are very old they would pick up a title like "Daddy" or "Granddad" or sometimes "Uncle" or "Aunt," even though there may not be any blood relationship.

Chapter XVI

CHRISTMAS TIME

December arrived and soon it would be Christmas time. They had the pie supper and cake walk to raise money for the community Christmas tree while Dick and I were in the cotton fields in western Oklahoma. They say they did real good raising money, so we should have a good treat sack for everyone on the tree.

Bobby and I had gotten our homework, so we were given permission to go out on the school stage and practice our part in the Christmas play that our room was presenting at the community Christmas gathering. We two had the longest parts, and we needed a lot of practice. While we were there, Jerry Branch burst out of the door of the room on the other side of the stage, yelling something back to his teacher. His nose was bleeding, and he was going to the well house to bathe his face.

Mr. Teague heard the commotion and loud laughing, but by the time he got there from our room, Jerry was gone and only Bobby and I were left sitting there. Mr. Teague had his paddle in his hand and had us to bend over the edge of the stage without giving us a chance to explain what had happened. We each received three licks from that big board. Neither shed a tear, and we were ordered back to our seats in the room. In all of my years in grade school, that was the only whipping I received that I didn't deserve, but a number of times I should have gotten one but didn't. So I guess it balances out somehow.

In a few weeks the big paddle disappeared. I had nothing to do with its disappearance, but I have to confess that I enjoyed it being gone. Rumor was that two eighth-grade boys slipped through an unlocked window during the weekend and got the paddle, tied it to a rock, and threw it into the cesspool at the girls' toilet. I was surprised, but it was never mentioned again, and another was not made to take its place.

The year following, Mr. Teague died with a heart attack. Perhaps that explains why he never replaced the paddle, because it hurt him to administer the punishment as much as it did for us to receive it. I remember one time that year when a whole bunch of us were playing dodge ball and lost our temper. It turned out to be a free-for-all; even the girls were involved. There were about twelve of us in the game, and we all were brought in and promised three licks with the big paddle. I was almost the last one to get his paddling (sometimes it is good to have a last name beginning with a W), and I remember how tired Mr. Teague was. None of us knew that he had heart trouble. Most of us knew he was a good teacher. He could make American history come alive, and he taught such things as white man's treatment of the negro and the Indians just like they really were. Many times our textbooks did not tell it like it was. For instance, it made General Custer a martyr, when actually his personal goal was to kill off all the Indians or run them from their land.

Our school was in the Chickasaw Nation of Oklahoma. We grew up to know the true stories about the Indians, as many of our neighbors were Indians, and I myself had some Indian blood. Several times during my childhood, I went to an Indian campground where they made stone instruments such as arrowheads, spear heads, tomahawk heads, etc. It was near a creek that was bluffed by flint stone. This is what they liked to work, because it would break and chip into the shape they wanted it in. Where they had worked, there was a large pile of flint chips, and one could find arrowheads, etc., that had a slight imperfection.

In the valley around the chip pile was a large number of earthen mounds. They were about twelve feet across and raised about a foot and a half above the valley floor. It was on those they put up their teepees. The mound kept them up in the dry during the rainy season. It had now been over fifty years since the plains Indians camped there, but the

161

evidence was still present to see and may be there to this day. Since then all those tribes were run out by the soldiers, and the Choctaws were moved in by force march from the southeastern part of the United States. Hundreds died on the long journey to Oklahoma. Many of the remaining Choctaws tried to build houses like the white man, but never could really adjust to white man's way of life.

Mr. Teague told us also of the slaves and their hard plight in life, of how the nation went to war over the way the black people were treated. Even after a war was fought and won, to set them free, they still, even today, have an uphill climb to obtain equality. I give Mr. Teague credit for all my teaching in human relationships. Even my father was a little weak in his philosophy toward black people. He just took the "let well enough alone" theory.

Mr. Teague even told us of the carpetbagger lawyers coming down from the north and cheating the five civilized tribes, whom the U.S. government had given the state of Oklahoma, out of their land. The Indian did not know the value of money nor the value of land, so they were talked into selling their two-hundred-acre allotment for just a few dollars. They only knew that a few dollars could purchase a new hat or a bottle of whiskey. Land had always been plentiful to them. If the wild game became scarce, they could always take down their teepees and move to new land. But now white man was rapidly taking ownership of all the land; when the Indian sold his allotment, there was no more land to go to. A few tracts were held by the tribe and controlled by the chief and could not be sold. It was referred to by the white man as "Indian Land." Those tracts still exist today, but most are under lease by white people if they are good for farming or pasturing.

Our Oklahoma history speaks of the great Land Rush of 1889 as a great thing in the history of the state but never mentioned that this was a large strip of land called the "Cherokee Strip." The federal government had given it to the Cherokee Indians to settle on and own "as long as grass grows and water flows," after their long trek from the East, where hundreds of them, pushed by the soldiers, had died before they arrived in Oklahoma. The land wasn't thought to be worth much until oil was discovered under it and huge lead and zinc mines were found. Some creek valleys were found to be good farming, and there were lots of buffalo whose skins were worth big prices back East.

Yes, I would say that Mr. Teague was a good teacher, and the school was a great loser when he had his heart attack and died. At least he taught us the truth about things.

After the panther scare a few weeks ago, some of us boys thought how much fun it would be to create the belief that another panther was prowling the little town. Joe helped us design the thing. We got a nail keg from Mr. Lewis. It was a hardwood keg that held one hundred pounds of nails. We got a piece of goat skin from Daddy. He had tanned it from the goat we had bar-b-qued last July 4. We stretched it over the mouth of the keg, like an Indian drum, and tied it real tight with a strip of rawhide.

From the center of the drum head, we tied a long piece of strong string. We hung the keg from some trees with cord and stretched the string out about two hundred yards. We rubbed the string with resin like we were ticktacking a window. We were about a quarter of a mile above town in the hills.

When we rubbed the string with a damp cloth, the roar out of the keg was unbelievable. It was far greater than we had thought it might be. Dick, Jerry, Fonze, and I were quite proud of the results. It sounded more like an African lion's roar than it did an American mountain lion, but we knew it was enough to bring fear into most hearts.

We rubbed the string about ten minutes, then stopped for the evening. The next day there was all kinds of conversation on what folks had heard, but most agreed that the mate to the black panther was prowling the woods above town looking for her mate. Doors were locked at night, and families took care not to let their children play out after dark. It was about a week before our keg was found by Mr. Jones, who was looking for a cow that had gotten out of the barn lot.

He brought our keg down to the little town so everyone could see what scared them. We boys were able to keep it to ourselves until Mr. Lewis remembered who he had given the keg to. And of course Daddy recognized his goat skin. He tanned and kept these skins to use to put new bottoms in straight chairs. He got a good laugh about what we boys did.

The story had been the talk in school, and the kids all rushed to see us and hear all about what we did and how we got it to roar like it did. Most of them had heard it and were frightened by it.

The big Christmas tree night came and preparations were made for the celebration. There was something that was bothering me, though. Billy Saulter (the Barn Haint) had remained a secret all year, but to think of his life all alone bothered me and so did the fact that Christmas was here and he would not get to celebrate it with the community and he had no family. So when the Christmas program was over and they gave away the treat sacks, I took an extra one without explaining to anyone why I did it.

When everyone gathered outside for about an hour of celebration, I ran as fast as I could go down the little road to Bill Williams' barn. I ran across the pasture in what was a real dark night. I was soon at the barn. I didn't know how I was going to approach Billy, but surely he knew someone had been doing good turns for him.

I yelled, "Billy!" as I approached the barn. At first I saw him run away from his fire out into the dark. I went ahead and approached his fire so he could see that it was just a boy. He slowly and cautiously walked toward me. I held out the Christmas sack. He took it, and I said, "Merry Christmas." He thanked me, and we talked a little while. I told him about his daddy's death and the fire that took the house and the sale of the property by the county. He couldn't talk plain because of the disease that he had, but I understood him just fine. He told me that he was going back to the institution. The winter was too cold, and he needed the treatment that they could give him there.

I left Billy that night at the barn and never saw or heard of him again, but I went home feeling good that I had shared a little bit of my Christmas with him. I guess there comes a time in all our lives when we begin to understand what Christmas really means.

On Christmas morning my house celebrated as usual. We were up early to open all our gifts, recognizing it was a little better this year than last, partly because of the wages Dick and I had earned in western Oklahoma.

We had a great Christmas dinner, and our whole family enjoyed the day.

Chapter XVII

OIL DRILLING BEGINS

Our Christmas vacation was soon over, and it was time to start back to school. The first day back Lowrance Allen told us of a company moving a large amount of drilling equipment in northwest of him.

We had known for a long time that our community sat on a fault line where there is a possibility of oil. Oil sometimes collects where the earth shifts from an earthquake, on one side of the fault or the other.

It didn't take but a couple days to build a derrick. It was a large one, so they could drill deep if they wanted to. But we had always been told that the land fault was about six thousand feet deep. It would stand to reason that if there was oil down there, it would be along that fault and about six thousand feet deep. For an oil well, that isn't very deep. I have heard that some are being drilled up to eleven thousand, and there's one out in New Mexico they are thinking of drilling seventeen thousand feet deep. That would be three and one-fourth miles deep.

Harry, Fonzie, Jerry, Dick, and I planned a trip after school up to where they were drilling. It was about a two-mile trip, and we planned to ride our bicycles. So at six o'clock, giving each time to finish chores, we met at my house, as I lived on the side of town toward the oil well. The derrick stood 120 feet high and was operated by a driller and roughnecks and supervised by a tool pusher. He is the one that told them when their bit was dull and needed changing. They were drilling through granite stone and a drill bit had to be removed about every other day. The pipe that held the drilling bit was called a drill stem and was fifty feet long. They would drill down the full length of a drill stem, then another was brought up and screwed on for fifty feet more drilling.

Mud was pumped down the center of the drill stem all the way to the bottom and forced back up the hole on the outside of the drill stem, bringing up the rock chips and stone grindings to be dumped out into the slush pit. These pumps were called mud pumps and would pump the mud at a high pressure. Sometimes the pump would stop up and had to be opened up to unstop it. When the head was taken off, mud would squirt everywhere. On a cold night like tonight, one would get soaking wet and had to change his clothes. A "doghouse" was provided for this purpose. An extra set of work clothes was always kept there to change into. It was also a good place to keep warm while the rig was drilling. Sometimes the well would drill a couple hours without roughneck involvement. Only the driller would have to be present to keep pressure on the drill bit, to continue to cut granite stone. There was granite down there because Oklahoma has the oldest mountain range in the United States. Much of it is rounded off from years of erosion, but most of it is buried deep in the earth from centuries of earthquakes. That is what created the fault that held the oil.

While the crew was in the doghouse, they would play dominoes or poker. We boys were invited to play with them. We would play dominoes, but had no money to play poker. Also, I was taught not to gamble, so playing poker was out for me. I wasn't even allowed to play marbles for keeps when I was growing up. I can honestly say I never lost any money gambling and am much better off for it.

About three evenings a week we visited the drilling rig to see how deep they had gone. In about six months they were down to the six-thousand-foot mark. We were there the night oil began to flow up through the mud and out into the slush pool. It carried a good pressure and looked to be a good grade of oil, almost clear, not black.

The next morning the tool pusher was called by the radio that was set up in the doghouse with the antenna up on top of the drilling derrick. Instructions were given to shut down drilling, which they did. It was Saturday, so we boys could be there. I thought I would get to see oil squirt out of the top of the derrick, but it never happened that way. Instead, they pulled out all the drill stem and had a company come in and plug off the well with concrete.

It took them about two days to tear the derrick down and fill up the slush pit with dirt. They loaded the derrick up on large flat-bed trucks and hauled it away. You could hardly tell where they had been. We were never told whether the oil was not sufficient to set up a pump and pump it out, or whether they were saving the oil field until a later date and the price of oil was higher.

Though they never told anyone, even the land owner, their findings and intention, we five boys were there when the oil flowed into the slush pit. So we always knew there was oil down there at about six thousand feet. We enjoyed the trips to the drilling site and the time spent in the warm dog-house or sitting between two of the large drilling motors. They put off a lot of heat, and some of the roughnecks would take a nap lying between them. When the driller needed them to put on a new drill stem, he only had to change the speed of the engines, and they would all come immediately to help.

For uneducated men, roughnecking was a good job. The pay was good, and they got to travel a lot. Some single men in our little town took up that kind of work and even went to Alaska, where they made big wages and in a few years came home and bought farms and homes.

Chapter XVIII

TURKEY JOHN GONE

A few days before Christmas, Turkey John came to town. He spent the night with us and gave Christmas presents to each of us. Mom gave John several boxes of .22 shells for his gift. After lunch John went down town and met up with some men who were drinking. It wasn't long before some of the men were picking on John. He never bothered anyone, but other men found a lot of fun picking at him. A couple men from the next little town took up for John, and a big fight occurred.

The fight was the worse I had ever seen. We lived across the street from the beer joint where the fight began, so I walked over to get a closer look. The fight got so bad, one of the men bit another man's ear off and they beat each other with clubs. John begged them to stop, feeling that he was the cause of it all. John got on his paint horse and headed home.

In about a week John came by on his way to Muldrow, Oklahoma. He had gotten a job from a rancher that he knew there, to take care of his cattle during the winter months. He was going to live in a line shack (a shack built on a fence line up in the hills). There would be plenty of wild game but no river close by for John to fish in. We never saw John again, but have since read a letter he had someone write to my mom's sister. He was home-sick and wanted to come back to Red River. He had accumulated some fishing nets, and he hoped some-day he would get to use them.

We got a letter from the county sheriff's department stating that John was partially buried by his boss and partially by the county. John had died like he chose to live, and that was all by himself. His dog, Bobang, was found dead lying next to him. The sheriff had found Mother's address in John's old hat band.

Though John had chosen to be alone, he was always present in my heart and mind. What he taught me about fishing and respect for wildlife never left me. As I grew to manhood, my love for fishing and hunting seemed to increase.

After the excitement of the oil well had ended, we all returned to the classroom. I had learned better how to trap for fur-bearing animals, so I began again running my daily trap line in Teague's woods to make some spending money. Each week I had a good bundle of hides to ship to Sears. Because of my trapping, I always had some spending money in my pocket. I always had money to go see the local high-school basketball team play and to go to Bokchito, which was the nearest town with a movie house. Most of their movies were westerns, starring Tom Mix or Gene Autry. Gene was my favorite, because he was a native Oklahoman. At one time he had worked as a telegraph operator for the railroad at Achille, Oklahoma, which was about fifteen miles west of where I lived.

Gene got his start in entertainment by getting acquainted with Will Rogers (who also was a native Oklahoman). They formed a group with Burl Ives and did a thirty-minute radio show in New York City. Gene and Burl sang, and Will told political jokes.

They all three went to Hollywood and got into the movies. Gene was the most successful of the three and owned his own film studio. After retirement he purchased a major-league baseball team.

I never lost my childhood dream of owning a big long car but had no vision of becoming rich. But most boyhood dreams never leave. After I was grown I went to the oil field in New Mexico and worked as a roughneck for a year or so.

After I spent my time in the U.S. Army, I entered college and graduated with a degree. In fact, both my brothers and I received degrees. All eventually got our master's degree. I took a job with Phillips Petroleum and worked for them over seven years. Then following the faith that my parents had taught me, I went into the ministry and pastored churches for thirty-two years before I had to medically retire. THE END